Underland

Warrior Stone Book 1

Best Wishes
R B Harkess

R B Harkess

Published by Metaphoric Media,
Broxbourne, UK
www.metaphoric-media.co.uk

Original artwork © Amygdala Design
(www.amygdaladesign.net)

(Originally published by Fox Spirit in 2014)

ISBN 978-0-9927861-3-7

For Ellie, who reads

Other books available by the author

White Magic: Warrior Stone Book 2
Aphrodite's Dawn
Girl at the End of the World (anthology)

Books as Robert Harkess

Maverick
Monk Punk (anthology)
Songs of the Satyrs (anthology)

ONE

Claire was already in trouble up to her hips, and if she missed this train her parents would ground her for life. After sneaking out to go to a 'Bleeding Black Hearts' gig, everything had gone horribly wrong. Now, she was barely half-way down the stairs when she heard the rails start to sing. The train was already coming in, and there was a good chance it was the last one of the night. She leapt down the rest of the steps three at a time, hung desperately onto the handrail as she swung around the corner, and ran out onto the platform. Her head spun, but the train was already there and she heard the familiar 'pop-hiss' of the doors starting to close. Diving through the nearest opening, she tripped and fell to her knees. The doors slid shut behind her with a clunk and the train moaned away into the tunnel.

She stood and looked around. Her cheeks were burning and she quickly checked her knees to make sure she hadn't holed her tights. A glance in either direction showed she was alone in the carriage, but the sigh of relief caught in her throat. She looked again.

Dim bulbs ran along either side of the ceiling instead of bright strip lights, and everything had a yellow tint to it. Leather loops rather than plastic-coated tubes hung down for people to hold, and the window frames were wooden, not metal. The floor was set out in parallel slats, with lots of little plugs of something stuck between them.

The train even sounded wrong when it pulled away, creaking and groaning as though everything was too much effort. It stank, not with the usual faint whiff of armpits and damp clothes, but with a stale smell of burnt tar and it took Claire a moment to realise the little plugs in the floor were actually cigarette butts. That's why the train smelt so bad. People had been smoking. Inside. Claire's nose wrinkled as she frowned.

The sounds of the motor and the wheels rattling on the rails were nowhere near as frantic as she was used to, and the carriage wallowed from side to side. It felt slow. Claire looked through the window of the door at the far end. It seemed she was the only person on the train. Her eyebrows shot up. There ought to be somebody else, even if this was the last one.

Her eyes opened wide. Maybe she had jumped onto some special engineering unit, like a test train, or a vintage train being used for a film shoot. Something 'period'. The smile faded as she realised she would get into trouble for spoiling the shot. It seemed whichever way she turned she was finding bother.

The train slowed and Claire hoped it was pulling into the next station. She could get off. With luck it wouldn't be where they were shooting and she could wait for the right train. Looking through the windows as the train burst out of the tunnel she realised the station looked wrong too. Like the train, there were no bright strip lights, just lots of old bulbs that looked as though they weren't getting enough power. Everything looked the same smoky yellow.

A sign flashed past but Claire was just able to read it. Fiddler's Green? There was no such station; at least, she didn't remember one, and she was usually quite geeky about such things. It must be the film set. She stepped back from the door and sank down onto a seat, waiting miserably for an irate director to yell 'cut' as burly security people threw her off the train and out of the station.

With an ear-torturing screech the train came to a halt and the doors opened. Somebody in a long, dark coat leapt inside, looking away from Claire and down the tunnel the train had come from. Claire stifled a squeal. She hadn't seen anybody waiting on the platform. The doors pop-hissed closed, and the person turned.

It was a girl, two or three years older than Claire, dressed in an outlandish collection of clothes that started with a leather aviator's cap and finished with heavy biker's boots. Beneath the long coat, either leather or waxed cotton, Claire glimpsed an equipment belt festooned with little pockets and gadgets, a tight fitting black top, and trousers with a black and grey camouflage print. Around her neck hung a pair of old flying goggles with blue-tinted lenses, and in her right hand she held something that looked like a ray gun out of a Flash Gordon movie. Dark hair frizzed out from the bottom of the cap and nobody would have described her as pretty. Claire thought the ensemble looked incredibly cool.

'Whoa,' the girl said. 'Who are you?'

'C-Claire.' She was mesmerised by this girl who could have been a crazy composite character from her favourite science fiction and adventure stories.

'Evie. What are you doing here? It's not safe.'

The train pulled away from the platform, then jerked and shook as though it had run over something. It kept moving, but the engine sounded very unhappy. Claire grabbed a rail to stop herself falling, but the girl just took a big step backwards to absorbed the sudden motion.

'Come on,' said Evie, her heavy boots thudding on the wooden floor as she ran past. Claire stared after, still uncertain, as she reached the end of the car, pulling open the connecting door and looking back over her shoulder. 'Hurry!'

Claire ran. There was an urgency in the girl's voice that scared her. Both doors to the next carriage were open now, and the floor bucked and heaved on the other side of the gap. Claire could see the tracks trundling past beneath. 'Take a big step,'

11

Evie yelled in her ear, over the wind noise and the clattering of the wheels on the rails. 'It's just like getting on an escalator.' Claire thought briefly of the signs she remembered seeing on these doors. 'Not to be used while train is moving. Danger of Death.'

The decision was taken away from her. She felt a hand in the small of her back, then a shove at exactly the right time to make her hop across the gap. Evie followed her, slamming the door behind her and fiddling with the handle. 'Go on,' she yelled as Claire waited for the next thing to happen. 'Get to the other end.'

Claire ran the rest of the way along the car and, on impulse, opened the next pair of doors. Evie flashed Claire a tight grin as she ran through. Whatever it was they were doing, the odd girl seemed to be enjoying it. Moments later they reached the lead car. Again Evie did something with the door handle before leading Claire to the front of the carriage.

'That should slow it down.'

'What?'

Evie flicked a questioning look at Claire, then glanced up and down her body. 'You aren't from around here, are you?'

Claire shook her head. 'I'm not even sure where 'here' is.' She looked back along the train, trying to see what they were running from, but they seemed to be on a curve that lasted for ever and she could see nothing further than one car behind them. The movie set idea seemed less likely and she was about to ask when the other girl spoke first.

'Oh, no,' Evie groaned. 'You fell through, didn't you? By accident. You weren't recruited?'

Claire shook, confused, scared, and starting to get angry. 'Look, what's–'

'*Here* is Underland,' said Evie. 'And that's a Morph. Well, that's what we call them.' She pointed back down the train. Claire followed Evie's finger along the now-straight cars and saw a hulking shadow lurching towards them. She took a step backwards.

12

'Keep it together,' said Evie. 'You've done pretty good so far.' She patted the gun with her left hand. 'Besides, this'll take care of him, if we can get him out in the open.'

Claire flicked her eyes from the wild girl to the shadow and back again, not quite sure which was the greatest threat.

'So where is this 'Underland'?'

'Underland is the place between the Real and Beneath.'

'Beneath what?'

Evie flicked Claire an impatient look. 'We live in the Real. The Morphs come from the Beneath. They want to find a way through Underland to get to the Real. We stop them.'

'We?'

Evie looked over Claire's shoulder. Her eyes narrowed and her lips tightened. Claire turned to see what Evie was looking at. The shape further down the train was getting closer and growing uncomfortably larger. To Claire, it looked wider than the aisle between the seats, and she was sure she could hear a ripping noise as it moved.

'Later,' said Evie.

They were standing at the most forward door and Evie turned away to look out the window. Something bright flashed past, and Claire saw her start to mouth a count down from five as her hand reached up to the emergency signal. Claire started to shout an outraged 'Don't'. Pulling the emergency cord for a prank would get them in big trouble, and she didn't want to add a fine to the grief she was already going to collect from her parents for being out so late.

As she finished drawing the breath into her lungs, she realised that the normal rules had probably been suspended. She reached out and grabbed hold of a pole just as Evie pulled hard on the bright red chain. The emergency brakes slammed on, and Claire saw the walls of the tunnel light up as sparks scattered from the screeching wheels. The train shuddered to a halt with only half the first car poking into the station. While it was still rocking on its springs, Evie threw the emergency exit lever and pulled the doors apart. 'Move it,' she called back as she leapt from the

13

train.

Claire cast a glance back at the rapidly approaching outline and jumped out after Evie. They ran through an arch and into a hallway where two wooden escalators rumbled up and away to the right. Dim globes of light atop poles between the stairs provided the only illumination. Evie tried to push Claire onto the one going up. Claire pushed back. She didn't trust the escalators, and couldn't see what was at the top. Besides, Evie appeared to know what was going on and Claire wasn't happy about walking away from that small reassurance.

'Go on,' said Evie. 'I'll be up as soon as I make sure it saw me.'

'What?' Claire thought the whole idea was to get away from the nasty shape chasing after them.

'I have to get it out into the open,' Evie replied. 'Then I can deal with it.'

Claire stumbled as she stepped backwards on to the escalator and steadied herself by grabbing the handrail. Evie flicked an impatient hand at her until she turned and ran up the moving stairs. At the top she stepped to the side and turned back to watch.

Evie was side-stepping away from the bottom of the escalators, craning her neck to see as much of the platform as she could. Sounds of metal tearing echoed up from the platform, then a crash. Evie fired her weapon then ran for the escalators. Too close behind her, a monster burst into the hallway.

The creature was about seven feet tall and blocky, with scaly skin that looked grey in the weak light. It stood on two legs, with heavily muscled arms that looked strong enough to rip a laptop in half the hard way. The head was like a crocodile - only the snout wasn't so long - and intelligent black eyes made it looked like a cliché bad guy from an anime. The Morph waddled, rather than ran, but it was fast and Evie was barely able to keep in front of it.

As she reached the bottom of the escalators, Evie spun around and brought up the toy gun. It spat a fast moving puff of something purple towards the Morph, missing its head by inches. Before checking to see if she'd scored a hit Evie started up the stairs. She had only reached the tenth step when the monster opened its mouth. Claire watched as the Morph's tongue, tipped with a ball as big as a baby's head, shot out like a frog's towards Evie's left shoulder.

The ball stopped six inches away from Evie's back. The air beneath sparkled and Evie lurched as if part of the force of the blow had connected. She stumbled into the side of the escalator, almost losing her footing but still scrambled upwards, half on her feet and half on hands and knees.

The Morph looked down at the red 'Emergency Stop' button mounted on a box and casually swung a fist at it. The box disintegrated, glass shards and sparks scattering outwards as the metal frame was hammered flat. Both escalators slowed and rumbled to a halt. Claire watched in horror as the Morph's mouth stretched opened again. Before she could yell a warning, the tongue sprang forward and thumped squarely into Evie's back. This time it truly connected and there was no sparkle in the air. It landed so hard Claire was sure she heard it, like a dull drumbeat.

Evie sprawled forward. Her arms flailed as she tried to try to protect herself and her gun was thrown though the air. She cried out in pain as her head cracked down on the edge of a step. Claire winced in sympathy. Blood ran down into Evie's eye from a cut. She turned herself over and faced the Morph as it climbed the stairs towards her. Claire looked around for anything that might help, but there wasn't even a fire extinguisher she could throw. Below, the Morph loomed over her new friend.

'Pus-filled bag of shit. Sod off,' Evie snarled, as she tried to scoot backwards, repeating the last two words over and over in a crescendo of anger and fear. Claire didn't understand Evie's predicament until - as if on cue - the Morph changed; blurring and bloating, becoming colourless and translucent. A bulbous sac extended from where its stomach had been, and sank

15

downwards. Evie tried to fend it off, screaming and cursing and beating at it with her fists.

Claire could hear a sizzling noise and a drum-like boom each time Evie hit the bubble, but as it sank lower Evie had less room to move, and then her arms were slipping through the bulging sac and inside the Morph.

Bile burned the back of Claire's throat as her stomach heaved. She took a half-step forward to go and help, then stepped back as she realised there was nothing she could do. The Morph dropped onto Evie and engulfed her.

Claire screamed 'No!' as Evie floated up from the ground, still struggling and twisting, until she was hovering in the middle of the Morph. The monster looked up at Claire and she clamped a hand over her mouth, realising too late that calling attention to herself was not her best idea. The Morph turned away as if dismissing her. As it moved off, it started to absorb its own arms and legs, stretching out until it looked like a slug with a bulbous head.

Claire couldn't see Evie's face, but she was struggling less and Claire realised Evie could be drowning in whatever gloop filled the creature. The Morph slid away towards the platform. Evie seemed to renew her struggling and slowly spun around inside the sac. Black splotches covered Evie's eyes and mouth, and for one horrible second Claire thought that something had started eating away at her face. A moment later, as the Morph passed one of the lights and Claire realised that Evie had pulled her goggles over her eyes and had another gadget in her mouth.

The Morph carried on down the escalator. Claire expected noise of some kind. Perhaps something gurgling or rasping like snake scales rubbing over themselves. There was a ticking sound, like metal cooling, but that seemed to be coming from farther away, out of sight. The Morph silently eased across the hallway at the bottom of the escalators and through onto the platform.

Claire was alone at the top of the stairs.

Two

Claire spun around, turning her back on the motionless escalator. Blood pounded in her ears and every breath felt like a conscious act. What had happened didn't feel like a dream - it was in colour, for one thing - but it was too weird. Had she only fallen asleep on the train? It would make things so much simpler if she had. She pinched her arm to try to wake herself up, but nothing happened except a red mark and some pain.

Four corridors led away from the top of the escalators; one each to left and right, and two directly ahead. The walls were tiled and didn't look too unusual apart from showing another unrecognised station name: Regent's Walk. Then she noticed something else missing. There were no adverts on the walls. Not even boxes for them to go into. There were always adverts; even back when they had done about tube stations and the war in history, the walls had been covered with them.

She looked again at the tunnels and wondered which she should take. If the station hadn't been locked up for the night she might find someone to help, assuming she could make them believe her. None of the tunnels bore any signs, so she picked the one to her right and ran.

The corridor went straight for about thirty yards then curved left. After ten more steps it opened out into a ticket hall. Claire skidded to a halt. There were no automatic ticket barriers, just a low metal railing with a two gates in it. The paint was pitted and flaking off, and the brass rail along the top was dull brown apart from bits where the brush of hands kept it polished and shiny.

On the other side of the railing she could see two brass-shelved windows in the wall, and next to them a door marked 'Private'. At least they didn't look too unfamiliar. Black shutters were pulled down over them, saying 'Position Closed'. Claire checked the other walls, looking for a ticket machine. There was no machine, and no sign that one had been hastily covered up.

Claire discarded the movie set idea, comfortingly normal though it might be. Special effects like the Morph didn't happen in real time; they took hours of post-production on powerful computers. This had to be real, somehow. She felt her hands start to shake and nausea burned under her breastbone. She took a deep breath and tried to focus on something practical, something useful. She had to find help.

She vaulted over the rail and ran over to the ticket windows, but as she got closer she noticed more things wrong. The window frames were all brass and wood; no aluminium or speaker grilles, no signs about assistance for the hearing impaired. She hammered on the glass anyway. 'Help! Is there anybody there? Please?' She tried the same at the door, pressing her ear against it, hoping to hear something. There was only silence. 'Shit,' she hissed, and kicked the door. 'ShitshitSHIT.'

A gate had been pulled across the exit. As well as a heavy metal lock holding the gate shut, a thick chain was looped around the two sides and was secured with a brass padlock as big as Claire's palm. She tried an experimental 'Help' though the grille, but she knew she was wasting her time. When the echoes of her voice finished ricocheting off the tiled walls, nothing more than faint susurrus came down the corridor to her; no road noise, no sound of people. She turned away and headed back to the top of the escalators. There had to be other exits she could try.

Every ticket office was abandoned, every way out was locked. At the fourth exit she tried, Claire started to heave at the grille, then kicked it, screaming at the top of her voice. The heavy padlock and chain ignored her utterly and she rested her head against the gate as she admitted defeat. She wasn't sure if it was her temper or her fear that got the better of her, but now she felt helpless. Forcing herself not to cry, she turned away from the exit and trudged back to the top of the escalators. Her hands were shaking and her knees wobbled with each step. Maybe there was something on the platform. An emergency phone, perhaps, or another way out at the other end.

She hesitated as her foot hovered over the first step. What if the monster was lurking on the platform? It might chase her back up here and she had already seen there was nowhere for her to hide. That meant sitting here all night on her own, and if the monster started to look around, she was still screwed. She took the first step, and felt her knee tremble as she put her weight onto it.

Halfway down was the odd-looking gun Evie had been carrying. Claire sat on the step next to it and picked it up, making sure the dangerous end was pointing away from her before carefully examining it. Despite its comic appearance, she had seen it do something and had to assume it could be dangerous. The trigger was obvious and right next to it a small switch pointing to a little red 'f'. The other position pointed to a green 's'. Other than that, it still looked like a toy, no more than a foot long and weighing no more than a grapefruit.

Claire almost let it fall back to the step, but decided to take it just in case. After flicking the switch from 'f' to 's', she pointed it towards the foot of the escalator and pulled the trigger. Nothing happened. It was either safe or a fake. She pushed it into her bag.

She stood and tiptoed down the rest of the escalator, ready to run if she had to even through she knew there was nowhere safe to go. Her heart was still hammering, but her breathing was even as she told herself 'don't panic' over and over again. There might be a cleaner, or someone else to get help.

Even if she did find someone to let her out, what then? She was still a dozen stations away from home. What good would it do to be out on the street in a part of town she didn't know? She had the money for a cab, but only from the last station, and she didn't have a clue if there was a bus she could take. Phoning for help would be just too humiliating.

Phone?

Claire slapped her forehead and dug a hand into her bag. It took a moment until her hand closed around the familiar shape and she pulled out her mobile. She pressed the wakeup button, dragged her finger around the screen to get past the security, and waited for the display to clear. Icons flickered into life and, finally, the signal strength indicator. It immediately turned red. Of course. No signal. That would have been too easy. She stuffed the phone back into her bag and stamped down the rest of the steps.

Four steps from the bottom she noticed a silvery sheen on the floor. Her heart leapt. Maybe there was a cleaner after all, with a mop or a polisher. As she got closer she realised it was a trail of slime, tracking out onto the platform. It had to be a trail left by the Morph that had taken Evie. Claire paused to curl her lip at how gross the idea was, then followed it across the small hallway.

She edged along the wall and peeked out onto the platform. Nothing moving, so she poked her head out for a longer look. The platform was clear. At the other end was a 'Way out' sign. Claire started to walk briskly towards it but as she passed in front of the train she took only took a dozen steps, each slower than the last, before she stopped and looked back.

Where was the driver? There was no slime around the front of the train so he hadn't been eaten by the Morph. And where had the driver been when they had stopped the train? Where were the police and the station staff, and everybody else who should have come running after a train was wrecked in a tunnel? And what about Evie? So there might be someone to help at the other exit, but how would Claire explain that a strange girl had been captured by an even stranger monster?

There was a wooden bench nearby and Claire took a seat right where she could look at the wrecked train. This might not be a dream, but it certainly wasn't real either. One side of Claire's mouth lifted slightly. If this wasn't her world, maybe she didn't have to play by the old rules, and be quiet little Claire with her nose in the books. In her imagination she had crawled through all the secret tunnels, she usually figured out the deadly trap before the hero did, and she fearlessly fought in every battle and avoided every ambush. She had always thought she could do as good a job as most of her heroes. Perhaps this was a chance to prove it.

She strode to the open door of the train and stepped into the first car. The trail of slime was about as wide as the aisle, so she hopped from side to side to keep her feet out of it. Morph had already pulled all the connecting doors off their hinges, so she didn't need to fiddle with locks and she moved quickly to the back of the train. Only half of the bulbs were working in the last car, but she could see that the farthest pair of doors had been torn out on the left side. One lay on the floor, folded almost in two, and the other was missing completely. The trail of slime went through the doors and vanished into the dark.

Claire stood at the hole in the side of the train and stared out into the tunnel. A lamp many yards along the tunnel wall shed some light and there was the dim glimmer from inside the car, but Claire couldn't see much outside. There was just enough light to ruin her night vision, yet not enough to actually see anything. She leaned against the partition beside the door and sighed. Failed already. No surprise there then. She stepped away from the door, intending to walk back to the ticket hall and sit next to one of the grilles until someone found her. If only she had a torch or something.

She stopped in her tracks, made an exasperated growling noise, and rummaged in her bag. Digging out her phone again she tapped and prodded it until it came to life and started

21

flipping around the menus. When her dad had given it to her for her birthday she had spent an entire afternoon searching through all the options and downloading new utilities and she was sure one of them… There it was. An app that turned the camera flash into a torch. She rushed back to the door and flicked the light on.

Outside was a narrow walkway, coated with slime. The harsh light from the torch cast sharp shadows and she couldn't be sure if what she could see was a handrail, or cables. Whatever it was, there was nothing between her and the walkway, so nothing to stop her falling to the tracks if she slipped.

Claire squinted at the gap, trying to figure if she could simply step across, or if she would have to jump. The torch would be draining the battery so she switched it off and pushed the phone into an outside pocket of her bag. She needed both hands anyway. Giving herself enough space for a 'run up', Claire took two quick steps and jumped.

THREE

The gritty wall gave no grip as her hands scrabbled across it. The slime was like oil, and her feet started to slip out from under her. Just as Claire accepted she was going to fall down to the electrified rails, the fingers of one hand closed around something solid. There was a handrail.

She pulled herself back to her feet, but as soon as she shifted her balance to take a step her legs tried to shoot out from under her. Jumping back onto the train would be impossible. She froze, eyes closed as she fought to steady her nerves and her balance.

When she opened them again, her eyes had adjusted better to the light and she could see a string of dim lights further down the tunnel. They turned the slime trail into a twinkling stream. She peered along the ledge, careful not to look back into the train, and saw that there were wooden poles on the far side of the narrow path, each with cables strung between them level with the top of the train.

With one hand on the handrail to her left, and the other holding onto a pole, she tried a cautious step. As soon as she began to shift her weight, her right foot slid forward and off to her left. Balance gone, Claire started to fall to her right and her other foot started to slip too. She pulled hard on the handrail, twisted, and let go of the pole. Terrified that she was going to end up under the train, she flailed with her other arm until her hand made contact with the handrail and she managed to steady herself.

It took longer to steady her racing heart this time. As she turned her feet from side to side, trying to get some form of purchase on the ledge, an insane idea came to her. She half-crouched, turned mostly sideways to the direction she needed to go, and moved her feet so one was slightly in front of the other. With one hand holding the rail and the other on a pole, she pulled. Claire slid forward on the slime, wobbling and almost falling, but moving. It was like riding a skateboard, only easier. She tried not to think of the goo sliding up over the toes of her new hi-tops, and scooted herself along again when the next pole came in reach. She stifled a giggle. It was fun, and she went faster and faster.

Until she lost her balance and slid towards the side of the ledge. She squeaked and got serious very quickly. The hand she kept running along the rail on the wall pulled her back to the centre and she set herself up again. Still with a silly smile on her face she slipped along until she saw a gap coming up in the walkway. Claire shifted her balance and tightened her grip on the rail to slow herself down.

The walkway dropped down three steps, rising up again after only a few paces. At the bottom of the steps, level with the track, was a door. It was the same dark and dusty brown as the tunnel wall, and it was open. Claire couldn't be sure in the dim light, but it didn't look as though the door had been forced.

The steps in front of her were coated with slime and looked treacherous. Claire thought about trying to put most of her weight on the handrail as she made her way down, but the steps were very steep. Reluctantly, she sat down and slid down each step on her backside, wincing at the clammy, gooey feeling of the slime seeping through her shorts and tights and reminding herself that a real adventurer wouldn't be so squeamish.

The sparkle of the slime turned left and went through the doorway. There were no lights on inside, and no light switch, so she plucked the phone out of its pocket and switched the torch on again, hoping the battery would last. The corridor was wide enough that she could find clean patches of floor, and she scuffed her trainers to scrub the worst off the muck off the soles.

Claire stepped from side to side where the slime was narrower, trying to stay on clean ground. The air was acrid with the sharp smell of ozone and hot metal, and there were many doors with vents in the tops and signs with lightning bolts saying 'Electrical Hazard'.

The corridor took a last left turn and stretched off ahead of her, no doors or junctions scarring the walls within the range of her torch. She kept walking, until a dark shape humped up from the ground at the edge of the light. Claire froze. Was it the Morph, waiting for her. She tried to cover her light with her hand, then realised it was a waste of time. If it was the Morph, it would have seen her.

Nothing moved. Claire counted to thirty, then started to move forward. She couldn't just stand and wait. The battery on the phone would go, for one thing. The mound slowly resolved into a pile of earth and beside it was an opening in the wall. It was oval, rather than rectangular, and not quite as tall as a normal door. Claire crept up to it and peered around the edge. The passage beyond looked as though it had been melted through the ground, rather than dug out, and she could see there was something transparent covering the walls. It was hard and smooth to the touch, and Claire guessed it had been made by the Morph, maybe from dried slime. Her top lip curled in disgust and she wiped her fingers on her shorts before she remembered they were already grosser than the wall.

The torchlight reached thirty feet or so along the tunnel, but again Claire was sure she could see something beyond it. Something that could have been another light. She turned her torch off to see it better, and a green glow shone softly along the whole tunnel. Her eyes adjusted to the softer light, and she

25

realised it was bright enough to use to walk along the passage. She tucked the phone into a pocket and tiptoed slowly along beside the slime trail.

The tunnel curved gently to the right and sloped downward. Claire tried not to think of how deep she was, or of all the earth piled above her, and it helped that the soft green glow wasn't bright enough to make out many details. When she had been in the man-made tunnels, the depth hadn't seemed to matter. She could trust in the implied strength of the concrete and steel she was surrounded by. Here, things felt different. Here she saw the raw earth around her, apparently held back by nothing. She looked up at the roof and felt the skin along her spine flinch.

The green light gradually brightened and Claire could see a lighter patch on one wall, as though whatever was making the light was shining through from somewhere else. A change in the way the tiny sounds she made echoed suggested that it was an opening into a larger space. She eased herself closer. The edge of the opening was smooth, glassy, and she wasn't sure how good the grip would be if she used it to lean against. She shifted her balance until she could ease her head around the edge of the opening.

Unless it was a really odd shape, Claire thought she could see most of the cave from where she was. It looked about as long a soccer pitch, although not so wide, and as tall as the sports hall in her school. Wooden boxes, some broken open, were scattered about, and there were blobs of jelly stuck to the walls. They shone with a sickly green light, and there were puddles of bright ichor seeping from them like thick dribbles of fluorescent snot. The floor looked unnaturally smooth and flat, like it had been worked on, and there were no rocks or boulders.

At the far end, at the very edge of what she could see clearly, Claire made out the blobby shape of the Morph, or if not *the* Morph then *a* Morph. Next to it was another, smaller blob that seemed to be floating in the air. It had a dark centre that made it look like a frog's egg, and Claire shuddered as she wondered if the thing was trying to reproduce.

She squinted and looked again. The dark centre was about Evie's size. The image of a fly wrapped up in spider silk popped into Claire's head. If this went wrong, she could end up in a sack next to Evie. Would she be kept for food? Or worse? What if these Morphs injected their eggs into unwilling donors, like a parasitic wasp? She felt sick and her hands started to tremble.

For a moment, the thought of looking for other exits from the top of the escalators again seemed like a much better idea than hanging around here, but the thought of going back out into the dark and slippery corridors with a torch that was probably about to run out seemed almost as dangerous as trying to rescue Evie.

Creeping into the cave, she dropped to her knees behind a crate tall enough to hide her. The gun still felt like a toy as she took out of her bag, which she put quietly on the floor before slowly edging to the side of the box. She lifted the gun and sighted along the barrel, aiming towards the Morph. It didn't feel right. The gun was too short to hold like a rifle, and there were no little ridges at the back and front to line the shot up. And the Morph was too far away. Even though she had a clear shot, the Morph was so close to Evie that Claire might hit her if she made a mistake. She had to rearrange things.

She ducked down behind the crate again, throat tight, hands barely able to keep a hold of the gun. She would have to get closer to the Morph, or get it to come closer to her. She dragged in three deep breaths then started to softly mutter a litany of heroes to bolster her courage.

She stepped out from behind the crate. 'Hey! Over here. Come get me if you can, blobby,' and she winced in horror as the last word left her mouth. Not cool. The thing flinched then started towards her, transforming into the Manga monster as it moved. Claire had almost forgotten the Morph could do that and she let out a real scream. But she still brought up the gun and pulled the trigger.

Nothing happened. She pulled it again and still nothing. The Morph had already covered thirty yards before she remembered she had put the safety on. She wasted more precious seconds as she fumbled for the switch. She flicked it up with her thumb and levelled the gun at the Morph. The monster was only twenty yards from her now, its mouth gaping and something squirming inside. She aimed and fired.

A tight cloud of purple shot out the front of the gun, missing the monster by feet. The weapon kicked back so hard Claire was knocked to the ground and lost her grip on the gun as she slid along the floor. The monster's tongue shot out and passed close enough above her head that she saw the heavy mass at the end. She thought it looked disturbingly like a clenched fist dipped in slime, and she felt a breath of air as it passed.

Claire looked to her right and saw the gun just beyond her reach. The Morph was almost on top of her now, snarling. She glanced up and saw a mouthful of sharp, pointed teeth. Its tongue was back in its mouth, but the mouth was still open and she saw something squirming inside. Claire waited a second longer then rolled right, towards the gun. The end of the tongue slapped onto the floor next to her with a noise like a raw egg breaking, then pulled back with a sticky rip. Claire grabbed for the gun, swung it around to where she hoped the now-howling Morph would be. She wasn't sure. Her eyes were closed in case she missed. She knew she couldn't avoid its tongue again, and had no wish to see it coming if this didn't work.

Her elbow hammered into the floor and the gun ripped out of her hand again. Had she pulled the trigger? For an instant she thought the Morph had slapped the gun away, but the snarl cut off with a popping noise and she was soaked by a waterfall of warm goo.

Claire wiped the slime from her face and tried very hard not to be sick. The goo was sticky and smelt of mothballs and dog food. She sat up, looked down at herself, and grimaced. It was everywhere. Luckily her mouth had been closed, but something was burning inside her nose and she did something disgusting she had only ever seen done by rugby players, once for each nostril. The burning eased, but the smell didn't go away. Her hair felt like she had gelled it too much.

28

Once she had slid to the edge of the pool, Claire carefully stood up. Goo oozed down her legs and tried to get under her sneakers, making walking tricky. Belatedly, she looked around for the Morph – just in case – but there was no sign of it. She shuffled cautiously up to the other end of the room.

Evie struggled inside the sac, but all she could do was spin slowly in place. As she tried to reach the side she rolled around to the centre again. The sac changed shape, and seemed to make Evie's rolling worse. Claire touched the sac; it was warm, perhaps even warmer than a body, and she had to fight down a surge of nausea at the thought the pod was in some way alive. She clawed at the membrane with her fingers, cringing at the touch.

The skin was too tough for her to make any impression on it with her nails, which were too short. When she tried to take a pinch of the membrane to tear it the slime on her hands made it slip through her fingers. She was getting nowhere, and slapped at the membrane angrily. Evie waved her arms, making her swing back and forth in the goo, then pointed to the floor before making a poking gesture. Claire nodded and started to look around. All the stones were rounded pebbles, but she found a splintered piece of wood from a broken crate.

Claire stabbed at the sack. It bent inwards but wouldn't burst. A slow shove was no more effective against the rubbery membrane. Eventually she tried a scraping motion, and the sharp point of the wood caught on a wrinkle that formed in the skin. The pod popped like a balloon. Gallons of disgusting gel spattered onto the floor and soaked Claire's legs and sneakers all over again.

Evie sat in the puddle, wiping the worst of the mess from her face before pushing up her goggles and taking something out of her mouth. She looked up at Claire for a moment and burst out laughing. Claire glared at her for a moment, trying not to find the situation funny but unable help stop herself joining in. The tension had burst with the pod, and now she felt it was either laugh or cry. Laughing seemed the more heroic option. They slid to the edge of the new pool, one on foot and the other sliding along on her backside, and at the edge Claire held out a hand to help the Evie up.

'Thanks,' said Evie, grinning. 'Good save.' She started to walk down the cave, scraping goo from her arms.

Claire looked at Evie's retreating back, mouth hanging open. Was that it? The ghoulish light made it impossible to see if Evie looked pale, and Claire could hardly demand that Evie held her hands out to see if they were shaking, but if Evie wanted to play it that cool Claire refused to be outdone. She took a few quick, careful steps to catch up and joined her. 'Sorry I made such a mess.'

Evie walked over to the gun and picked it up. When she looked back at Claire, her face had lost its bravado. 'You did a really brave thing coming down here.'

Claire felt her eyes prick and her throat tighten. Partly because the whole situation was suddenly a bit too much to cope with, but also because it was rare that anyone near her own age said anything good to her. 'I didn't know how else to get home.'

'Doesn't matter. You came,' said Evie. They had reached the entrance to the cave, and Claire picked up her bag. When she looked up she saw Evie was giving her a speculative look. 'You'd be a hell of a good Warrior, you know. I can't believe you were never recruited.'

Claire felt herself blushing and looked away for a moment. She wanted to ask 'recruited for what?' but as usual her tongue had already stuck to the roof of her mouth, stealing her words. She used the state of her clothes to change the conversation to something safer. 'I look a mess. What will my mum say?'

Evie laughed again. 'Don't worry, this will all disappear when you go back to the Real.'

'You mean this is a dream?' asked Claire, a leaden block of disappointment appearing in her gut.

'Oh no,' said Evie. A tight, feral grin curled her lips and her eyes seemed to shine. 'This is as real as our world and twice as nasty. The damage is permanent, and the cuts and bruises are still going to hurt. You haven't seen the tiniest slice of Underland. I meant what I said, though, you would make a great Warrior.'

The a thrill of excitement tingled through Claire but the fear of exposing herself, of opening herself to another person, squashed it. One careless, honest comment had cost her years of being shunned. She embraced Evie's words, warmed by them, but couldn't trust that they weren't just for the moment. She settled for a noncommittal shrug.

Evie looked surprised, then disappointed. 'Never mind. You'll forget all about it in few weeks.'

'Doubt it.'

'You will. That's the way it works. Memories of this place are… slippery.'

Claire let out a half-hearted chuckle. 'Isn't everything?'

Evie grinned. 'Good point. If you don't keep coming here, though, it fades from your mind. Probably best for you in the long run. So how did you get here?'

Claire explained about the gig she had sneaked out to, and how bad the band had been, and the crush at the station and how she had hidden in a toilet because she felt too many of the wrong sort of people had been watching her. About how she had nearly missed the last train and got dizzy and fell through the doors, all the time trying hard not to get too embarrassed as Evie's grin got wider and wider.

'Awesome,' she said when Claire had finished. 'Not the band. Bleeding Black Hearts are shit, really. I meant the whole trip thing. You've got the guts. So, do you want to go back to the real station, or home? At the station I can drop you the instant you left, or if you want me to drop you at home, you'll get there now.'

It didn't make a lot of sense to Claire, but she just wanted to get in, keep the argument with her parents as short as possible, and sink into a hot, bubbly bath as quickly as she could.

'Home, please.'

FOUR

Maths class was usually something Claire enjoyed – or at least didn't mind. Or she hadn't until the geek squad started acting like she had grown an extra head.

She was used to being ignored. The 'A Team' blanked her because she wasn't stick thin and didn't wear designer clothes. By definition, she could never be their version of cool, and because she stuck up for herself if they tried to bully her, they simply decided she didn't exist.

The geek squad she had never understood. Logically, she should have fitted right in. They should have been her sort of people. It wasn't a big group, two or three girls from each year, but it still made no sense that every one of them should stop talking to her simply because she had once dismissed a vampire romance movie as soppy rubbish rather than a real vampire story.

That left the Goths and Emos, and the Dweebs. Whilst she would never be intentionally mean to a Dweeb, she didn't have anything in common with them, and the Emos were too self-obsessed and depressing. That left the Goths, and she didn't have the nerve. She loved the look, and the music, but felt intimidated by them.

So Claire had wandered through school on speaking terms with most, but with no real friends. Largely ignored, which suited her fine. Until she had gone to that stupid concert. She never really had the nerve to brag about it, because there was nobody to speak to. Without someone to share the confidence with, there was no way to get her heroic act circulated without doing it herself, and that said 'look at me' so loud it looked desperate. All she had got out of it was a tee-shirt that didn't really fit and a pointless month-long grounding. She never really went out anywhere, but her parents had felt they needed to take a stand.

But the one thing that had changed was the geek squad. It seemed every time she turned around at least one of them was watching her. If there were two, then they covered their mouths or hid their faces and Claire just knew they were talking about her. It had started off as being mildly amusing, but now it was starting to get irritating.

Melanie Styke was the worst of them. She was above Claire, in Year 11. Whenever Claire caught Styke watching her, the girl was scowling. It was disturbing and aggressive and Claire hadn't a clue why. Admittedly, it was Styke she had argued with about vampire romance, but that had been three years ago.

So lessons with too many geek squad members in them were no longer fun, and neither was lunch. It seemed that wherever she tried to hide herself, someone would find her, and she would be subject to surreptitious glares and stares as they tried to make it look like they weren't watching her.

Today, when the class finished, Claire stuffed her books into her bag and hurried to her locker. Lunch and her e-reader swapped places with her schoolbooks and she slipped out of the school's main building and into the grounds. She wouldn't embarrass herself by breaking into a run, but she hurried. The best places to sit filled up quickly. The prime locations were always dominated by one group or another, depending on how secluded they were and what the group was intending to get up to, but Claire was happy if she could find somewhere that was

34

quiet. She only wanted to read and munch in relative tranquillity, and you could waste the whole break looking for the right spot.

There was an empty bench around the corner from the doors to the toilets. She curled her nose, but the bench was on the girls' side so it probably wouldn't smell. She strode purposefully over and planted herself in the corner so she could put her back against the wall and stretch her legs out along the bench. Ear buds came out of a pocket and were plugged into the e-reader. She tried to immerse herself in her reading so she could ignore the two girls from Year 8 that had decided to sit under a tree only forty feet away from her.

The quality of the light on the screen of her e-reader changed subtly. It wasn't quite a shadow, but somebody was standing next to her. Claire scowled, hoping whoever it was would take the hint and go away, but the sense of presence remained. Eventually Claire tapped 'pause' on the e-reader to stop the music, twitched a bud out of one ear and looked up to deal with the intrusion.

It was a girl. She had a cocky grin on her face, but she looked out of place. A moment later Claire realised that the girl didn't belong at her school. She was wearing a uniform of sorts - grey jumper over a white shirt, a grey skirt that was way too short, and thick black tights – but the lack of a tie and the heavy boots would both have got her sent home and earned her a deferred detention. Still, there was something about her that looked familiar. Perhaps it was the wiry hair.

Whatever it was, the girl seemed to know her.

'Shift the legs, Claire. Lemme sit down. We need to talk.'

Not quite sure why, Claire slowly drew up her knees to make space at the end of the bench, and popped the other bud out of her ear. It seemed typical, and at the same time deliciously ironic, that the only kid in the school who wanted to talk to her wasn't even supposed to be there. She tried to get her right eyebrow to go up on its own. It was something she practised in the mirror, and it worked about one time in six. The other five she looked an idiot and, remembering this, she settled for raising both. 'We do?'

The older girl gave her a hard look as though she was searching for something, then she saddened as though she hadn't found it. 'Damned memory leak,' she muttered.

Claire was impressed. Most people couldn't get away with saying something like that and still look serious.

'I need you to think really hard, Claire,' said the girl, looking straight into her eyes in an uncomfortably intense way.

'About six weeks ago, you went into London. To a gig.'

Claire nodded, eyes narrowed. This wasn't common knowledge, but it wasn't a secret either. 'So?'

'What happened when you left?'

'I went home. And caught a pile of trouble.'

'In more detail.'

'Why?'

'Humour me.'

Claire felt her forehead crinkle. She wanted to move back from this child of weirdness, or at least look away, but there was something in the girl's eyes. They were grey, with a black band around the outside of the cornea, and Claire found herself wishing she had cool eyes like that.

'Focus. What happened when you left the gig?'

'I went to the underground station and caught the train.'

'Is that all?'

It seemed really important to whoever this person was, so Claire concentrated and tried to play the night back in her head. She remembered the crap music, the crowd, waiting for the crowd to clear, and the spooky men leering at her. 'Pretty much. I hid in the toilet for a while, then ran down to catch my train.' But there was something else, something hiding just behind the peripheral vision of her memory. Her frown got deeper, and she saw the look of disappointment on the weird girl's face get more intense. There was a hint of desperation there, too.

'What was the next station the train stopped at, Claire?'

A name popped into Claire's head and she almost said it out

36

loud before she realised there was no such station. She tried again, but the name stuck. 'Fiddler's...?'

The older girl's face lit up, mouth twisting into a lopsided smile. Claire pushed a finger into each temple and rubbed, and felt like she was popping a mental zit. Her memory spat forth an image of the girl in front of her, but wearing a weird hat and with a pair of goggles dangling around her neck and -

'Evie?'

'Yes!' The older girl hissed, grin turning savage for a moment as she made a tight punching with her right fist, then the expression collapsed into one of relief. 'Shit, but you had me going there. I was beginning to think you were too far gone.'

Claire was about to ask what Evie was talking about, then she remembered their last conversation. 'Oh, the memory fading away thing, right?' Then she felt her mouth gape and her eyes open wide as everything else started to flood back into her mind.

Claire covered her face with her hands, eyes tight shut and unable to breathe as her muscles locked. Evie slid from the bench and knelt next to her, putting her hand on Claire's shoulder and squeezing gently. 'Hold on. It only lasts about a minute. You'll be OK.'

Images flashed and flickered in her eyes, smells tingled in her nose. Claire took her hands away from her face and saw they were trembling. She put them on her knees and let her breath out with a whoosh. 'How could I have forgotten?'

Evie gave Claire's shoulder a last squeeze and moved back to the bench. 'That's the way Underland works.'

Claire turned and put her feet on the floor. She noticed that there was only one geek squad spy watching her now. Even from a distance she looked agitated, which in turn made Claire feel uncomfortable. It took her a moment to realise Evie was talking again.

'... a Warrior.'

'I'm sorry?'

'I know. It's amazing, isn't it? I had to argue with the council for hours until they agreed, but I finally beat them down. The job is yours if you want it.'

Claire groaned inwardly. Evie looked pleased, proud and excited, all in one, and had obviously just told her something she thought was incredibly important. And Claire would either have to make her rewind and start again, which would look really rude, or act like she didn't care. Rescue came in the unlikely form of Melanie Styke, striding around the corner with another Year 10 girl in tow. She was, as usual, turned out in full skirt and blazer, with her prefect pin perfectly placed on her left lapel.

'I don't know who you think you are, but you are not supposed to be on these grounds and unless you leave this school immediately I'll be forced to report this... to... a...'

The finger Styke had been vigorously waving in front of Evie slowed and stopped as she caught up with what her lieutenant was whispering frantically in her ear. She sniffed, frowned, then backed away a step. The two Year 8s hovered a few feet away; far enough out to keep out of trouble, close enough to hear every word. 'Yes, whatever.' Her bluster level picked up again. 'You are still not supposed to *glerk*.'

Evie had risen to her feet and taken four quick steps to put herself right in Styke's face. The prefect had tried to back away, but Evie had been too quick. She grabbed Styke's lapels in her fists, turned and shoved the prefect into the wall.

'Do *not* speak to me like that,' said Evie. She hadn't hit Styke with the wall hard enough to hurt, just firmly enough to make a point. Her voice was dead and level.

'Wha? But? You can't—'

'Do this?' Evie pulled her back and hit her with the wall again. 'I can and I will because I'll bet that you are supposed to be the Recruiter here, eh? What was your name? Shite, or something?'

'St-st-styke.'

'That's right. I looked it up before I came.'

'Who-?'

'Start with 'why?'' Evie suggested, giving the lapels another shake.

'Why?' Styke agreed.

'Because I want to know how you could have been so damned stupid as to have missed one of the best prospects I've seen in years.'

'What, her?' Even pinned against the wall, Styke still managed slap Claire in the face with her contempt.

Evie cocked her head to one side. 'Surely you aren't referring to the drop-through who actually managed to track a Morph and rescue a Warrior. Don't tell me you are so far out of the loop that nobody told you that story.'

'Look, she isn't one of *us*,' Styke said, an edge of desperation in her voice. 'I knew she had been down. We could smell it on her. So we followed standard procedure and watched her.'

'Standard procedure is that you refer any possible candidates to the SFU for approval and possible contact.'

'Yes, well, she's too old now anyway,' Styke shot back, sounding more confident and trying to prise Evie's hands off her lapel. Evie gave no ground.

'Really? You need to jump in occasionally and actually pick up on the news, because if she's not one of us,' Evie drew the word out sarcastically, 'then how come she is being offered a provisional direct entry as a Warrior?'

Styke froze, and there was a collective gasp. 'They can't do that,' Styke hissed, and Claire couldn't miss the hateful, jealous glare that Styke favoured her with.

'I talk fast,' said Evie, smiling in an entirely humourless way, 'and I bullied them into it.'

Styke's body sagged as she gave in to the inevitable. 'Who are you?'

Evie grinned, letting go of Styke's lapels and giving them a gentle tug to settle them back into place. She fiddled with the Prefect pin, making sure it was perfectly aligned, then put her face uncomfortably close to Melanie's. 'The name,' she paused, 'is Jones.'

A susurration of whispers broke out around Styke's little band of helpers and they took a collective step back. Melanie

39

swallowed so hard Claire could see her throat working. 'Evelyn Jones? *Warrior* Jones?' Evie nodded, grinned with the same warmth as a tiger, and Styke's face went very pale. Evie gave her blazer one more pat, then sat down next to Claire again.

'That's right, so if you people wouldn't mind, I have a job to offer here and I would rather do it in private.' Most of the group had disappeared before Evie had finished speaking. Only Styke seemed intent on dragging her heels, but even she eventually turned and walked away. Evie waited until she was about to turn the corner at the end of the wall before she called out to her. 'And Shite—'

'That's 'Styke'.'

'Whatever. No teacher running around the corner in five minutes, and no messing with Claire. You understand me? Fully?'

There was a hint of rebellion in Styke's eyes, but it faded and she nodded once before walking away. Evie leaned back against the wall and chuckled. 'That was fun.' She looked over at Claire and her face fell into a defensive semi-pout. 'Come on, Claire. The bitch should have picked you out years ago, or reported you to whoever had the job before her. Let me guess. You don't get on? Something personal?' Claire nodded and Evie looked smug. 'Thought so. I can spot her type every time. Still, maybe you won't have to worry about her any more, eh?'

Claire looked at Evie, head cocked to one side. 'Why?' Then she realised that Evie must be talking about whatever it was she hadn't heard before Styke interrupted. 'I'm sorry, I think I missed something.'

'Keep up,' said Evie, shaking her head. She stopped and looked intently at Claire. 'How would you like to be a Warrior?'

Claire's mouth opened, but her brain had nothing to pass on. The whole idea was ridiculous, unexpected, impossible. Wasn't it? She realised she was staring at her hands and quickly raised her eyes to look at Evie. The older girl looked disappointed, and embarrassed, like a friend who'd given you an awkward birthday present. The bell for end of break chose that moment to ring. 'I have to go,' said Claire, looking down, feeling relieved that she didn't have to answer right then.

'Is that a 'no'?' Evie asked.

'Not 'no', but...' Claire took a deep breath. 'It's unexpected. I only just got my memory back. This on top is overload.'

Evie nodded. 'I understand. You'd be trained. By me. They wouldn't throw you out on the street.'

'I have to go.'

'Can we talk again? Today?'

Claire was on her feet, edging away. She wanted to pass on the offer, but part of her that needed to know more. And Evie was looking at her like a puppy that had been told off and Claire didn't have the heart. 'Remember where I live?' Evie nodded. 'This evening, seven o'clock. Wait at the gate, out of sight. I'll make up an excuse to come out.'

Evie nodded, but Claire was already turning away and hurrying to her locker. She was going to be late for History.

FIVE

The rest of the day had been a disaster. The geek squad hadn't said a word to her, but there had been a major increase in background muttering and pointing. It had been impossible to concentrate. Her memory seemed determined to keep playing that absurd night over and over, adding more detail each time it did so. No matter how hard Claire tried to focus, her attention had wandered about like a butterfly. She even had 'words' from two of her teachers before the afternoon was over.

Things were no better when she got home. Her mother, in an act of superhuman self-sacrifice, had cooked her microwaved sausages with mashed potatoes and baked beans. Claire smiled, thanked her devoutly vegetarian mother for polluting her plastic gloved fingers with processed dead animal flesh, and tried very hard to eat. Her appetite was as delinquent as her concentration, but she made a point of eating all the sausages.

Later, in the lounge, Claire fidgeted her way through the news. Seven o'clock took forever to arrive, but with ten minutes to go Claire still hadn't thought of a decent excuse for going out. Eventually, she decided on simplicity and honesty. 'I feel all antsy,' she said, rising from the couch she had been sharing with her father as they watched the TV. 'I'm going to go for a walk.'

43

'Good idea, sweetie,' her mother enthused. 'Blow the cobwebs out. I swear by it. Just be careful on the road.' Claire turned quickly to keep the unavoidable smile hidden. Her mother's head had been filled with cobwebs and dandelion fluff since Claire could remember, and so far there was no sign of it blowing away. Still, Claire loved her for it. She opened the front door and waved her hand outside. It wasn't cold enough for a coat, so she snibbed the latch and pulled the door closed behind her.

The sky was spring blue, dotted with candyfloss clouds edged with pink from the setting sun. Her trainers made a satisfying crunch as she walked down the gravel drive to the gate, and she sounded like a squad of soldiers marching in parade. A head poked briefly around the edge of the hedge, but Evie pulled back too quickly for Claire to wave at her. When she got to the gate, Claire looked back at the house and decided to take a chance. 'Quick,' she called, softly. 'Over here.'

Evie moved smartly around the corner and the two of them set off at a jog. Claire called a halt seconds later as the house disappeared behind the barn on the edge of the yard. Evie leaned against the wall. She had dropped the bogus school uniform and was wearing camo pants and a dark top with a deep 'V' neck. Claire could see a pendant hanging around Evie's neck. It was a complex pattern of wires coiling around a wooden frame and in the middle was a dark red stone. It looked home-made. Claire stood a couple of steps away from the barn and flicked a glance at Evie's face. The older girl looked as nervous and edgy as she felt.

'Nice place,' said Evie. 'Farm?'

Claire shook her head. 'Used to be. We converted it, sold off of most of the land. We kept a couple of the smaller fields and we rent them to people with horses. Dad says it's to keep a gap between us and the developers. My mum uses this for her 'craft shop',' Claire pointed at the barn they were hiding behind and rolled her eyes.

'Sounds cool,' said Evie.

Claire knew she was only being polite and shook her head. 'She not very good. Most of the stuff she sells is made by other people, but it makes her happy, I guess.'

An awkward silence fell. Claire couldn't look Evie in the face, and Evie seemed to be fiddling with a splinter of wood sticking out the side of the barn. 'So what did you want to talk about?'

'The offer, obviously.' Evie's voice was snappy and Claire took an involuntary half-step back. Evie pulled a sour face. 'Sorry. I'm not very good at this sort of thing. Look, remember I said you would make a good Warrior?' She waited for Claire to nod. 'Well, after I brought you home that night, I got to thinking. We're short of Warriors. I guessed you wouldn't want to start at the bottom, so I went to the council and argued with them, and got them to agree that you could come in as a sort of 'direct entry'. If you wanted to.'

Claire started to answer, or got as far as opening her mouth to trot out the speech she had ready. How she had thought about it, and whilst it had been exciting in a way, it had also been really scary and dangerous and she didn't think it was a good idea. But the words wouldn't come out. She looked up and saw Evie's face turning pink, the look of disappointment coming back, and Claire wondered what it had cost Evie. What it had cost her to come and ask, and what it had cost her to arrange this deal.

'I'm not sure,' she said, honestly. 'Do I have to say yes or no right now? There seem to be a million questions I should ask first, and I've only got a half hour before they wonder where I am.'

Evie looked flustered for a few seconds, then her face lit up and she snapped her fingers. 'I'm an idiot. How about I show you? Or start to, at least?'

'How?'

'Let me take you there. We can have a look around, and you can ask questions until your lips cramp.'

'In thirty minutes?'

Evie's smile got even wider. 'Your folks won't even know

45

you've gone. Promise.'

Claire looked right into Evie's eyes, trying to keep the scepticism off her face. Evie met her gaze squarely, and Claire shrugged. 'Alright.'

Evie moved, standing so close beside Claire that she could feel Evie's body heat through her sleeve. Evie linked her arm through Claire's, latching on tight. 'Once you get the hang of it, it'll be a lot easier. So all we do now is walk forward, quickly. Ready?'

Claire wasn't sure that she was, but nodded anyway. Evie gave a count of three, and they stepped forward. On the second step, without warning, Evie pulled Claire hard to the left and spun her around. There was a dizzying moment of vertigo, and Claire was stumbling as she fought to keep her feet under her.

'Easy,' said Evie, keeping hold of her arm. 'Just stand for a moment, get your balance back.'

Evie's voice sounded wrong, echoing like they were inside and Claire realised she had her eyes screwed tight shut. She opened them, slowly, and felt giddy all over again. They were in a large room with a checkerboard pattern of tiles on the floor and a matching pattern on the wall facing them. Evie, still holding on to her arm, gave a gentle tug.

'You OK? We need to get off the pad.'

Claire took a deep breath, looked from side to side, and let the breath puff out again. 'I guess so,' she said, and let Evie lead her towards a door. 'So where are we? Are we in this 'Underland'?'

Evie nodded. 'Thought you might be able to tell. Doesn't the air taste different?'

Claire experimented with the idea, breathing through her mouth, then her nose. There was something, metallic and smoky, but so slight she could have been imagining it. She shrugged.

'This is the SFU—' Evie started. Claire interrupted her straight away.

'SFU?'

''Special Facilities Unit',' Evie explained. 'It's who we work for down here.'

'And what do we do?' asked Claire, and when there was no immediate answer she looked up to see a half-smile tugging at the corner of Evie's mouth. She was about to ask what the joke was when she realised she had said 'we', not 'you'. Now *there* was something to think about.

'Later. Let's get you some basic kit first. Don't want to go out naked.'

'Pardon?'

'Local slang. Sorry.'

They walked along a corridor. It looked much like any other corridor in an old building, like a stately home or a museum, but there was something not right about it and it took Claire several minutes and a flight of stairs to figure out what it was. 'Are those gas lights?' she asked, pointed at one of the sconces where a ball of yellow-white light bobbled behind a fluted shade of frosted glass.

'No, not gas,' Evie said, a grin hovering around her lips, but she didn't say anything more. Claire pouted at her back and followed her to a double door. A sign pinned on the right hand door said 'In: This Side ONLY'; hand written in elegant copperplate and neatly underlined several times. Evie pushed the other door open and stepped inside, her gait changing to an insolent swagger. Claire followed, using the right door.

The room was enormous, filled with shelves and racks that seemed to go back as far as Claire could see. Ten feet from the door was a counter that stretched the width of the room, and from which thin iron bars rose to the ceiling. There were three serving hatches built into iron frames along the counter. Only one was open, and behind it stood something slightly shorter than Claire, with wrinkled grey skin and eyes like a goat. Its ears were tiny, and an arc of ridges and bumps ran around its eyes like spectacles. Its hands were surprisingly small, with only three very dexterous-looking fingers.

'Jones,' it said. 'Predictable as ever. Surprise me one day by

47

coming in through the same door as everybody else.' The voice was dry and the consonants all seemed to have a click in them somewhere. Claire felt Evie nudge her with an elbow and realised she was staring. She pasted a smile onto her face and tried to look friendly.

'New?' said the thing behind the counter, jerking a pointy chin in the direction of Claire.

'You could tell?' said Evie, tone sarcastic. 'Probably a trainee.'

'Probably?' Ridges moved on the creature's face, either side of its eyes, and Claire guessed that it had done the equivalent of raising its eyebrows.

'Long story I can't be bothered to tell you. You should have her in the books; look under 'Stone, C'. I think her number is 2149.'

'2146,' the creature corrected. 'Basic equipment?'

'And a Kevlar. And a locker.'

'Size?'

Claire realised they were both looking at her, and blushed. 'What size?'

'Any size, so long as it's yours,' said the creature behind the counter.

Claire reluctantly admitted to being a 12. The door over the serving hatch slammed shut and the creature walked away. Claire looked at Evie and raised her eyebrows, but Evie put a finger to her lips. Claire was to wait. The creature returned in a few minutes carrying a cardboard box about two feet long by a foot wide. On the top was a clipboard with a form on it. The creature put the box on his side of the mesh, opened the door, and pushed the clipboard through. 'Sign this.'

Claire took the clipboard, looked carefully down the list of eight items, and handed it back. 'No. Not until you hand over the box so I can check it against the list.'

The silence that followed seemed to last minutes, and the store-thing's slit pupils bored into Claire's as if challenging her. Then it barked a loud 'Ha', and slid the box through the hatch.

Claire checked through the box, checked the list, signed, and handed the clipboard back.

'At least she has a brain,' it said, looking at Evie, then it turned back to her. 'I am Krosset, storeskeeper. You need anything else, you come to me. With a requisition. Your locker number is 23.' He slammed the hatch door closed and walked off into the depths of the racking.

'That was odd,' said Claire.

'At least he liked you.'

'He did?'

'Of course.' Evie pulled a wry face. 'Sorry. I'm not making a good start as a teacher. Krosset is a Grenlick. It's really rude to ask a Grenlick for their name, and they only offer it if they don't think you're a waste of space. If you don't know, or you if you aren't sure everybody with you knows their name just call them 'Grenlick'.'

Claire nodded, trying to take everything in and store it as Claire led her down another corridor and into a room full of metal lockers. There were eight rows, each twenty lockers long, and there were long wooden benches set along the walls. Claire's locker was at the end of the room, and the door was already open. Evie showed her how to set a new combination using a gadget on the back of the door that looked like an exploded clock. Claire pointed at the box.

'How much of this stuff do I need right now?'

Evie rummaged, taking out a long coat, a pair of goggles, and something on a leather cord. 'Just these for now.' She looked at Claire with a critical expression. 'Should have thought this through a bit more, I suppose. But I'm not on duty. We'll be OK.'

Claire looked at Evie, then down at herself. She was wearing black leggings and ballet pumps, against Evie's grey camo pants and heavy boots. She put everything that wasn't needed into the locker and closed it before picking up the cord. On the end was a pendant, just like Evie's, except it looked less worn and the red ball in the middle was the bright red of fresh blood, rather than the dark wine-red of Evie's. 'What is it?' Claire asked, lifting the chain over her head. As she went to lower it, she saw the number 2146 engraved into the back.

'Put it against your skin,' Evie advised. 'It's the most important thing you can own down here.' She walked away, back two rows, and disappeared down an aisle. Claire slipped into the coat, pulling a face at how heavy and stiff it was, then picked up the goggles and followed. As she turned into the same aisle, something flew towards her. She had no time to duck or catch, and was resigned to whatever it was hitting her on the head when it bounced away, still a foot from her. Her skin tingled softly where it touched the back of the amulet. Evie grinned at her from behind a locker door. The number on the locker, seventy-seven, stuck in her mind.

'The amulet is a Personal Protection Device. We call them Kevlars. Think of it as a kind of stab vest.'

'Stab vest,' said Claire, then winced as she hear how shrill her voice sounded.

'Come on,' said Evie. 'Let's get out of here. I know a great café not far away. My treat.'

Claire nodded. They left the locker room and followed a maze of passageways until they reached a more substantial looking door. Evie touched a brass plate, which glowed a warm yellow and there was a loud click from the lock. Evie grabbed the handle and pulled.

The first thing that Claire noticed was that there weren't enough colours. Everything was washed out. Not as bad as the monochrome orange of a street light, but a similar blandness. She looked up at the sky. It was an insipid off-white that had no texture. The next thing she noticed was the mountain.

'"W...w...?' she gave up and pointed.

'Mount Primrose,' said Evie, her mouth twitching as she tried not to laugh. You think that's bad, look behind you.'

Claire turned, stumbled, and gasped. 'But that's the Tower of London,' she blurted. 'We were just in the Tower of London? What's it doing here?'

'Mostly the Tower,' Evie agreed. 'But look again.'

Claire did. 'It's different. It's too big, and some of those buildings shouldn't be there.'

'And that's Underland in a nutshell,' said Evie, jerking her thumb along the path to indicate they should get moving. 'It's just alike enough to let you think you know where you are and what you are doing. But it's not London. Remember that.'

SIX

They walked through a checkpoint and out onto the street. The road wasn't as busy as she would have expected from 'her London', but the pavements were still crowded and the road was full of traffic. Only it wasn't people on the pavement, and the traffic wasn't cars or trucks. Some of the smaller vehicles looked like flivvers out of old silent movies. The larger stuff all seemed to be carriages and carts - just without the horse. Instead, they had things that looked like miniature steam engines, but running on rubber wheels and with no chimney. She shook her head and looked away, realising she was gawping like a tourist and hoping that Evie was going to start with the explanations soon.

The buildings looked old, but not unremarkable, and she caught sight of a road sign that told her they were on Great Tower Street. The foot traffic melted out of their way but Claire didn't miss the sideways glances, suspicious and distrustful, that stirred in their wake. Evie dragged her into a quieter road, Harp Lane, and halfway down they found a small café. There were some tables set up in the street, unnecessarily sheltered under white umbrellas.

Evie gestured that Claire should take a seat at a table away from the road, then knocked on the window before sitting opposite her. It was a polite tap, and within a minute the door opened. Claire felt a pain in her ankle and realised Evie had kicked her. She had been gawping again. The being standing in front of them was easily seven feet tall and looked somehow rectangular, like the Easter Island statues. She wore a pale blue smock, sleeveless and ankle length, belted at the waist with a thin cord, and the waitress' pad she was holding looked ludicrously small in her over-sized hands. On her feet were sandals, held in place by thongs.

'Good day, Warriors. With what might I serve you?

'Good day, Sa,' Evie replied. 'A pitcher of squash and two glasses, if you would?'

'It will be my pleasure. Chilled?'

Evie smiled and nodded. The waitress gave an abbreviated bow from the waist before turning and walking back into the shop.

'You've really got to stop that,' said Evie.

Claire was about to ask what when she realised she knew perfectly well. 'Sorry. It's all so – unexpected.'

'Get a grip. Underland isn't safe, Claire. It's not a theme park. That's why you have the Kevlar. We're still kids, but we do a very grown up job here.'

'Start there, then. What does this place need us for, and why not adults?'

'Because as you get older it gets more difficult to drop through. I've got another two years, maybe three. My snapback will get shorter first, and then I won't be able to get in at all. Three months after that I won't even remember I was here, and I wouldn't believe it if I wrote it down.' Claire saw sadness pull at the corners of Evie's eyes, and must have let it show on her own face because Evie made a brushing-away gesture with her hands.

'Will you forget it? Really?'

Evie's face suddenly looked haunted. 'I'd bloody well better, because I am terrified that a part of me deep inside will remember this place, and somehow I'll still miss it.'

'You like it that much?'

Evie nodded, then made an obvious change back to the original subject. 'They need us because humans are the best there are at detecting Morphs as they break through, and then tracking them down. And we have a certain amount of protection.'

'I thought you said it was dangerous,' said Claire, then sat back in her seat when Evie glared at her interruption.

'We recruit kids with weirder imaginations, usually around ten years old. Oddly, more girls than boys. Not too many. Not even from every school. They get some training and acclimatisation topside, then they come down here. They get more training, and serve duty as runners. If they last, they make Observer. There are Observer stations all over the place, every city, every region. If they get a sighting, a breakthrough, a runner gets sent to a Warrior. The Warrior goes to the incursion site, tracks the Morph until she can burst it.'

Claire pulled a face. 'That sounds so gross.'

'The alternative is worse. We don't know how they do it, but if we don't get them, then a Morph can ascend and get to the Real.' She put up a hand as Claire tried to interrupt again. 'No, not as a monster. They change, become something like a virus or a ghost. They infect people, and change them.'

Claire started to laugh, but choked it off when she saw a naked fury in Evie's eyes. 'No joke. Nobody knows why they do it, but the hosts become detached, disinterested in the people around them. Cold. Dysfunctional.'

'That's... Why doesn't somebody do something about it?'

'We are.'

'I mean for real. Police, or scientists, or something?'

'Excuse me, Constable, but this person has been taken over by a creature from the Beneath, who is making them a less-nice person,' Evie spoke in a sing song voice, and her eyes were mocking. Claire pulled away a little. There was so much anger in the older girl, and it seemed she didn't always know where to direct it. The waitress chose that moment to come out of the shop, breaking the spell. She carried a tray, and from it she placed two tall, thin glasses onto the table, followed by a pitcher of something pink with a foamy top. As though she sensed the tension at the table she looked curiously at both girls, but said nothing and departed after offering them another slight bow.

Claire waited to see if Evie would make the next move, but the older girl was looking down at her hands. She was gripping the edge of the table so hard that bloodless crescents showed under her fingernails. Claire picked up the pitcher and poured a half-glass for each of them. Evie still didn't seem ready to speak, so Claire lifted one of the glasses and sipped cautiously at the contents. It was delicious, with a texture like a cross between a milkshake and a smoothie and a flavour like strawberries. She struggled very hard with an urge to gulp the rest of the glass down and grab for the pitcher, and kept things down to another controlled sip. Claire decided she would give Evie another chance to get it together, then she would ask to be taken home, and then was surprised by how disappointed that decision made her feel. 'So, can we eat everything here?'

Evie jumped. Her face came up and her expression was one of bewilderment, as though she had been kicked out of a daydream. 'What? Oh, yes. Pretty much. Apart from Grenlix food. Think twice before taking anything from a Grenlick. And Angels, too.'

'You have Angels here?'

'Yeah,' said Evie, but her mischievous grin was back. 'With Grenlix, you don't know where the food has been, or often, what it was. Angel's, you've got to wonder why he's giving you anything.'

'So you don't trust Angels?'

'I don't trust anybody. Not even you. I know you're good in a fight, and you don't spook too easily, but apart from that I don't know who you are.'

'So who, what, was the waitress?'

'Hrund. Nice people usually, especially the ladies.'

'And I call her 'Hrund' if I don't know her name?'

Evie blanched. 'Crap, no. Not unless you want to be thrown out, or over a wall. Everybody else its 'Sa' for females and 'Ser' for males. And don't touch anybody.'

'What?'

'Don't touch anybody, even through your clothes if you can avoid it. Didn't you notice everybody getting out of our way?'

'Well, yes, but–'

'It hurts them. All of them. Think of brushing up against a radiator. Just a touch and you pull your hand away and go 'ouch'. Press your hand against it and you burn, right? I don't know how or why. I do know that not all of the Underkin are happy when they see one of us walking around, so try to stay out of their way.'

Claire poured the last of the squash into her glass, pointedly ignoring Evie's scowl. There was a low thrumming noise that had started to interfere with the conversation. Claire looked over her shoulder to see what it was, but the street was empty so she settled for leaning closer across the table.

'So what's this deal you are supposed to be offering me.'

'Exactly what I said. Fast-track Warrior.'

'Why?'

'I told you; you're good.'

'And the rest of it?'

Evie squirmed on her seat, looking years younger as she understood she had been caught out. 'How did you know?'

'Styke. She was–' Claire tried to find a better word, but had to settle with what she first thought of. 'Shocked.'

Evie nodded. 'That's true. It's never been done before.'

'Then why?'

'Because there aren't enough of us,' Evie said after a pause that made it obvious she didn't want to answer. 'Not enough Warriors. More and more Observers bottle out, or get locked out before they can graduate. We can't recruit as many kids. People pay more attention, so there's not as much freedom as there used to be. You're a natural. With some training, you'll be near as good as me, and a damn sight better than most.'

The thrumming noise was so loud now that Claire waved her hands next to her ears and shook her head, telling Evie to wait. In reply, Evie pointed upwards. Claire looked, and gaped. An airship was coasting majestically overhead. Claire couldn't help but think of the opening of a certain movie where the big spaceship chasing the little space ship just gets bigger, and bigger, and bigger. An engine nacelle went directly over them; Claire couldn't guess how big the propeller was. Her sense of scale was out of order. The whole nacelle tilted and the thrumming took on a deeper, more powerful tone as the airship began to pick up altitude.

'Freighter,' Evie yelled. 'Probably heading south to Greater Germany.'

The rumble started to fade as the airship turned lazily to port, still rising. Claire watched it until it left her line of sight, then turned her attention back to Evie.

'The whole place is like that,' said Evie, her eyes shining. 'Please, just say you'll do the training. For three months. Easter break is around the corner, so it's an easy start and you can pull out whenever you want. Try it.'

'How do I find the time? I can't keep disappearing for hours without reason.'

'It's not a problem. There are some things I can't tell you. Not until you've joined the program. You'll just have to trust me.'

Claire stood up and pushed her chair back under the table. Evie looked up at her, head tilted slightly sideways, face hopeful. Claire shrugged as casually as she could.

'Where do I sign?'

SEVEN

Back at the SFU headquarters, Evie took them in through a different door and up several flights of elegant stairs, until they ended up at the end of a very long corridor. At the other end was a double door, and a Hrund stood on either side. Claire guessed they were male because they both had ridges over their eyebrows and the waitress hadn't. Each wore black knee length smocks with red belts, and held a six foot long staff. They nodded formally as the girls passed and, after a perfunctory knock, Evie led them through the doors.

A female Hrund sat behind an oversized desk, on top of which were three neat piles of paper and a oversized manual typewriter. She looked up at Evie, smiled, and indicated a row of chairs with an elegant, sweeping hand gesture. 'The director will be free in five minutes, Warrior Jones.'

'Thank you, Sa,' said Evie, nodding her head politely. She pulled Claire towards the chairs as the secretary's fingers started a staccato tap-dance of the over the typewriter keys. Evie was whispering in Claire's ear almost before they sat. 'We're going in to see the boss. Absolute top dog. Even when he gives you his name, call him Ser. He's Sathaari. They can get really pompous. Bow when we leave. Piss him off and your life will be miserable forever. And he doesn't like me.'

'So why are we going to see him?' Claire asked.

Whatever Evie had been going to say was lost in the rattle of the two doors being thrown open and a bustle of people leaving. There were handshakes all around, mumbled pleasantries, and Claire tried to remember not to stare. It wasn't easy. There were five in the group, all apparently male. Two looked so ordinary Claire would have passed them in the street and thought them human. One was taller and more heavily built than the other, and he was obviously the senior of the two. They wore old fashioned clothes, like either they were Victorian or going to a fancy wedding. At least they had some colour in their bright ties and fancy waistcoats.

The other three looked stretched; tall, thin and out of proportion. Their faces were long and doleful, and broader at the top than at the chin so they looked triangular. Claire couldn't figure out if their eyes were too big, or if the nose and mouth were too small. They wore bland frock coats in black with charcoal grey trousers and black boots, and looked like undertakers. Evie nudged her. She realised that she was staring again and averted her eyes, but not quite quickly enough to miss the calculating look the human-lookalike boss flicked at her, and then the longer stare he directed at Evie.

The group broke up. The secretary, who had emerged from her behind her desk as soon as the doors had opened, escorted four of the group out of the office whilst the one who was left disappeared back into the private sanctum. Claire glanced at Evie and saw she had a calculating look on her face. She nudged Evie's arm and, once the girl was looking at her, raised her eyebrows.

'That was Natrak Sum. Wonder what he was doing here. He'd have no business–' Evie broke off as the secretary walked back to her desk then nodded towards the door.

The room was dark and stuffy. Even though there were two tall windows at the far end, the décor seemed to ingest any natural light and only allowed the dim glow of the wall sconces and table lamps to have any effect. The walls were panelled in dark, polished wood, which made everything draw in still more.

Furniture crowded into the room. The centrepiece was a large desk, easily five feet across, which looked to be made of the same dark wood as the walls. To one side of the desk were two comfortable chairs and a couch clustered around a coffee table. On the other were a larger table and six chairs. Evie steered them to two plain chairs in front of the desk, and they came to a halt between them.

The person behind the desk shuffled things around and peered at papers. Claire wondered that anybody would still try to use the trick, it was so old. It was supposed to make you think you were unimportant, or at least less important than other things the person on the other side of the desk could be doing. Claire thought it made him look stupid.

'So, Jones. This is the *exceptional candidate* you have been trying to bully us all about?' The papers stopped shuffling and Claire found she was being peered at over a pair of half-moon spectacles.

'Yes, Ser,' Evie answered. There was a tension in Evie's voice, but Claire hadn't heard a reason for her to get mad yet. The person behind the desk turned his attention to her.

'My name is Aslnaff. I am the superintendent of the Special Facilities Unit. Jones has persuaded,' he paused, and his mouth puckered into a little moue of disagreement, '... us all that you are sufficiently gifted to be granted an expedited path to the position of Warrior.' He paused, sniffed, and used the middle finger of his left hand to push his glasses back up the bridge of his nose. 'I remain to be convinced.' Each word was extravagantly enunciated, and crisply bitten off. 'However, the rest of the Council seem to find merit in this endeavour, so I am compelled to trial it. You are therefore granted a status of 'Provisional Warrior', for a period of three months only after which you will be assessed and the continuation of said position and status re-evaluated. You are entitled to the protection due any human member of the SFU, and access to such reasonable equipment as your instructor deems appropriate for your training. Do you agree?'

Claire nodded before he had really asked the question, and then was not really sure why she had been so hasty. Surely there were things she should have been asking this man? Person? He slipped a sheet of paper across the desk towards her, with a pen atop it. 'Sign.'

Claire leaned forward and picked up the pen. Aslnaff's hand was already extended, waiting to take back the signed sheet, but Claire put the pen aside and lifted the paper closer so she could read it in the poor light. Aslnaff sat back in his chair and she was sure she heard a muttered 'well, really'. The form was written in some form of high legalese, and ninety per cent was incomprehensible. The gist seemed to be that they would help her out where and when they could, but that she was in this of her own choice so if she got hurt it wasn't their fault. It didn't surprise her. She needed to get her parents to sign similar cop-out's when she did just about anything with the school.

She looked at Evie, eyebrows raised, to make sure that this was what the older girl was expecting. She got back a non-committal shrug. Reaching out, she picked up the pen and tried to sign, but was rewarded only with dry scratching. Evie coughed and looked pointedly at something on the desk, and Claire blushed as she dipped the pen into an inkwell before trying the signature again. She put the pen down next to the inkwell, and handed the paper back to Aslnaff. He tossed it onto a pile without looking at it and turned to Evie.

'Very well, Jones. She's your problem now.'

Claire felt the heat rising in her cheeks again, but Evie grabbed her by the arm and twisted it slightly forward before making a small bow herself. Claire somehow managed to do the same, then Evie was dragging her discretely towards the door. As soon as they were outside and the doors were closed, Evie gently pushed Claire against a wall.

'Calm down. He was deliberately trying to wind us both up. Take a breath.'

'But why?'

'Because he's Sathaari. They're all stuck up and rude. Or maybe because he can. I warned you he didn't like me. That's why he just called me 'Jones'.' She was shaking her head now, and had let go of Claire. 'I can keep myself from blowing up at him, but it's hard. He was really, I mean really, against the whole idea of training you up. It was so cool pushing this past him.'

Claire heard a muffled noise and looked up to see the secretary unsuccessfully trying to control a smile. Were they funny, or was it funny they were showing no respect to the boss? And was she just some kind of trophy Evie was using to annoy Aslnaff? She adjusted her coat. A couple of deep breaths had settled her, and now all she wanted to do was get out of the office. 'So what's next?' she asked.

'Next,' said the secretary, 'we add you to the security system. If you would place your hand here?' She gestured to a copper plate mounted on top of an ornate box right at the corner of her desk. Claire did as she was asked. There was a gentle warmth and the plate glowed with soft yellow light. A moment later, the glow had expanded so that it covered Claire's hand. She was about to jerk it away when she heard the secretary say 'That's fine.' She lifted her hand. The glow seemed to linger around it for seconds, and it wasn't really clear if it faded away, or soaked in. She remembered her manners and looked over at the Hrund. 'Thank you, Sa.'

The secretary smiled warmly. 'My pleasure, Warrior Stone.'

Claire managed to keep it together until she had her back to the secretary before the huge grin spread across her face. It had a hell of a ring to it. That was when she looked up and saw Evie looking at her, wearing an equally wide smile. Claire's smile faded, thinking that Evie was mocking her, but there was no malice, just warmth. Evie jerked her head towards the door and they set off through the bowels of the building again.

'So the tall thin guys are Sathaari. Who were the others? I mean, they looked so like us.'

63

Evie's face darkened. 'They're Angels.'

'I thought Angels were good guys.'

'Try Angels as in 'of death'. Wherever there is a crooked deal, there's an Angel behind it or at the bottom of it. They're plain nasty. I mean, nobody would trust a Grenlick very far, but Angels are devious. Nasty.'

'So there are no people here except us?'

'A few. Very, very few. There are more in the United Americas, supposedly, but not here.'

They were back in the locker room. 'What's next?' Claire asked.

'Getting you home.'

'What? But I've only just got here. I don't want to go home yet.'

'You've been here nearly three hours, and I have no idea what your snapback tolerance is yet.'

'There you go again with the 'snapback'.'

Evie signed. 'It's complicated. There are two ways to get out; jump or snapback. A snapback takes you back to the same time in the Real as when you jumped in, but you can't come back until you've caught up.'

Claire was frowning so hard it hurt, and her mouth made word shapes but nothing came out. 'That doesn't make any sense.'

'It does if you don't want to meet yourself here. Anyhow, it's time to go home. You'll crash as soon as you get there, I promise.'

Claire pouted, opening her locker, and putting her coat and goggles inside. She was lifting the amulet over her head when she felt Evie's hand on her arm. 'Not that. I mean, you're supposed to, but don't. The rules say no Underworld tech in the Real, and some say it makes jumping more difficult.'

'So why do I leave it on?'

'Because sometimes you have to jump through in a hurry. You may not have the time to come here, and the Kevlar is your most basic protection. Your only protection. Nobody takes them off.'

Claire let the amulet fall from her fingers. Questions crowded to be asked and there was so much that still didn't make sense. But Evie said it was important so she left the Kevlar on and closed the locker door. She started to turn away, but stopped when she felt Evie take a hold of her arm. 'Stand still, facing your locker. Look at it. Hard. Fix it in your memory. When you come and go, you need to have the picture real in your mind. If you can fix this in your head, you can save yourself a lot of time walking here from that stupid room with the patterns.'

Claire tried to fix the image of the door in her mind, and was about to ask Evie how long she had taken to get the hang of it when she felt Evie's leg behind her as something pulled her around and twisted her...

...right back to where they had been standing behind her mother's barn. Claire staggered and took a step sideways before she caught her balance, and she glared at Evie. 'I wish you would stop doing that.'

'Easier to move you when you aren't expecting it.'

A wave of fatigue washed over Claire and distracted her from making any snappy comeback. Evie looked sympathetic. 'I tried to warn you.'

Claire opened her mouth to argue, but Evie raised her hand. 'No, no more rules or questions tonight. We can start again tomorrow.' Tomorrow was Saturday and Claire saw her habitual weekend lie-in fade to a wish.

'When? And where? Here is no good. Mum works in the barn all day and I'm not supposed to hang around unless I'm helping.'

Evie thought for a moment. 'We need to be somewhere you know really well, but where there won't be too many people.'

Claire grinned. 'Do you have a library card?'

EIGHT

Claire was sipping an apple juice when Evie stomped into the little café in a corner of the library.

'I thought I mentioned 'not too many people'?' Evie offered as a greeting.

Claire glanced up from her e-book. Evie was towering over her and looked grumpy. She was wearing her usual warrior outfit but without the gadgets. Claire had dressed more appropriately this time; a pair of second-best black jeans, a green tee, and her walking boots. 'Good morning,' she replied, her voice pointedly bright. 'Do you want anything?' She gestured at the café.

Evie shook her head. 'Can we just get on?'

Claire shrugged, put her e-book away and finished her juice. By the time she stood up, Evie had her arms tightly folded and was drumming the fingers of her right hand on her left arm. 'Come with me,' Claire said, deliberately making her tone cool.

She led them to the back of the library and down a flight of stairs that had a seldom-used mustiness about them. At the bottom was a very plain door with a panel of frosted glass in the top. The odour of age and infrequent interest got stronger as Claire pushed the door open. Just inside was a battered desk, equipped with the usual office clutter and a delicate brass bell. Claire picked the bell up and rang it softly.

A distant voice muttered, 'Coming, coming,' and shuffling footsteps scuffed closer to the desk. An archetypal fusty librarian appeared from between two stacks, wild hair and wire rim glasses pushed up over his forehead.

'Morning, Mr Lee,' said Claire, raising her voice. The librarian's face crinkled into a smile.

'Good morning, Miss Stone.'

'School project. We need to dig around the archive.'

'"Dig around *in* the archive",' he corrected absently and nodding. 'Of course. Remember to sign yourselves out when you go.'

Claire leaned over the desk. 'Will do, Mr Lee.' She put only her name into the register, and signed herself out an hour in the future. 'This way,' she said to Evie, pointing off into the darkness.

Automatic strip lights flickered on over their heads as they walked to the back of the archives. They saw nobody else and other than their own footsteps they could hear nothing apart from the faint shuffling and muttering of the librarian, far in the distance.

'This quiet enough for you?' Claire asked.

'I guess. Can I get down here on my own?'

'Don't see why not. Just tell Mr Lee you are working on a project with me.'

'Suits me. Ready?'

The sudden switch caught Claire off guard. 'For what?'

'First lesson. I'm guessing that you are going to have a problem getting in and out so you have to practise. It's going to be a pain if I have to fetch you all the time.'

Claire bit back a sarcastic apology for being such a burden. She had the feeling that Evie wasn't far off having a row with someone, and she didn't fancy being the target.

'Jumping works differently for everybody. You just have to pay attention when you get taken through, then find a way to

68

make the same thing happen for you. It's kind of like making your mind turn a key in a lock. Or throwing yourself at the ground and missing.'

Claire recognised the quote instantly, but didn't think Evie knew it came from a book. She was sure it wouldn't improve Evie's mood to know it wasn't original. She stood still while Evie came close to her and grabbed her arm, and tried to concentrate as Evie made the odd little twist in a direction that wasn't there. An instant later they were in front of Claire's locker. Evie let go and quickly stepped to the end of the row.

'You didn't focus on where you were going,' Evie snapped.

'I was trying to see what you did.'

'You have to do both.'

Claire sighed and opened her locker. There was more within than when she had last looked. 'Santa's been,' she said, trying to decide if she liked the delivery service or resented that someone else could get into her locker so easily.

'Krosset must have heard you signed up and shipped in the rest of your kit. You don't need all of it today.'

Claire put on her coat then rummaged through the box that had been left on the locker's shelf. The utility belt looked fun, but when she lifted it and looked enquiringly at Evie, the other girl shook her head. Disappointed, she let it fall back in the box. The goggles she put in a pocket, then found what looked like a torch. She found the switch quickly enough, but started turning it over in her hands and prising at the seams with a thumb nail.

'What are you doing?' Evie asked.

'Trying to figure out where the batteries go.'

Evie laughed, but there was a sharp edge to the sound and Claire felt she was being poked fun at. Still, it was better than snappy and surly. 'It doesn't have batteries,' said Evie. 'It runs on magic. Like everything else.'

Claire froze, glaring at Evie. 'That's not funny.'

Evie raised her hands defensively. 'I swear. Everything here, one way or another, works on magic. Or what they call magic. We'd probably call it something else, maybe all scientific, but

69

they call it magic.'

'So we have to do spells and stuff to make anything work?'

'We can't *do* magic – unless you count jumping. Nor can Hrund. Nobody is quite sure about Angels. We just get to use magical stuff.'

Claire was on the edge of asking to go home. If Evie was going to be this much of a cow for the next three months then it didn't matter how cool it sounded to be a Warrior, it wasn't worth it. But when she looked up she saw Evie was looking open and honest, and wasn't trying to hide a smirk or a lie. 'But there's no such thing,' Claire said, and it sounded lame as soon as she said it.

Evie shrugged. 'It's how things work down here, and it seems to do what they say it does. I'm not going to argue. What I understand is it's like a magnetic field, but magic. Things can store magic like batteries and recharge themselves from the field. Heavy duty magic is collected Outside and tankered into the city for factories and cars and stuff that uses too much to take it from the general field.'

'Magic tankers?'

'I'll show you one, someday.'

Evie walked down the room to her own locker. Claire followed and stood next to her as she put on her equipment belt and stashed a number of small items in various pockets.

'I wouldn't stand there if I were you,' Evie commented, casually.

'Why not?' Claire asked, but Evie had already flattened herself against her locker. Claire felt a brief tingle, then was pushed sideways. She landed on her backside and slid several feet along the floor. As she looked up to protest, a young man flickered into existence in front of her, standing in front of the locker next to Evie's. Evie had her hand covering her mouth but Claire could tell she was laughing. At her. Again. The young man looked at Evie, confused, then turned to see Claire on the floor. He flushed bright red and held out his hand.

'Sorry. Guess you must be new.'

70

Claire took his hand and let him pull her to her feet before they all backed out to the edge of the room. 'My name's Jack. Jack Cooper, Senior Observer.' He had his hand out again, this time to shake. Claire took it briefly. It was warm and dry and he didn't try to crush her hand with his grip, which was nice. She guessed he was about the same age as Evie, just short of six foot tall, and quite slim. He wasn't particularly handsome, and his darkish hair was a total disaster. He had nice, dark brown eyes, and a friendly smile.

'Claire Stone, trainee Warrior,' she replied. It still felt weird in her mouth as she said it and from the way his eyebrows shot up, either Jack was surprised or he had already heard of her.

'Pleasure,' he said. 'You should watch out for that. Someone jumps into the same space as you, it'll shove you out the way..'

'I was just going through that,' Evie interrupted, her tone frosty again.

Jack gave a rueful half smile. 'Of course. I'll let you get on with... whatever...' He turned away and walked off.

'That was a bit rude. Is he someone I should be careful around, or something?' Claire asked.

Evie shrugged. 'He's an Observer. Could have been a Warrior, but turned it down.'

Claire didn't know what to say. Perhaps that was the way things were here. Perhaps it was just Evie, or Jack. She decided to wait and see, and went back to her earlier question. 'So what are we doing for the rest of the day?'

Evie scratched somewhere under her coat. 'Not sure. We should keep it to six hours or so this time. We need to find out where your snapback limit is.'

'So we're not going to practise jumping in and out?'

'Not this trip.' Evie rubbed her chin and looked thoughtful for a moment. To Claire, it looked contrived, like Evie had known all along there was going to be a 'sudden change of plan'. She worked to keep any expression off her face.

Evie face cleared as though she had just had an idea. 'I think we should go out for a wander.'

71

NINE

'Anywhere in particular?' Claire asked.

Evie shrugged. 'I dunno. Maybe introduce you to a few people you should know.'

They walked down to the bowels of the building and through another door with a brass identity plate. More stairs, and then they were on a short, dimly lit platform. Evie went up to an ornate brass button, and pushed it.

'Private station,' she explained, yelling into Claire's ear as a train roared through at full speed. 'Don't worry, the next one will stop for us.'

As promised, the next train squealed to a halt, and Claire finally had an explanation of why the driver hadn't raised the alarm on her first trip to Underland. The cab at the front of the train was empty. The platform was only long enough to take the first car, and only the first pair of doors opened. They got on and Evie took a seat while Claire stood and studied the map over the doors. She tried to speak over the noise of the train as it picked up speed. 'What-?' was all she got out before Evie gave a pointed cough. Claire looked around and saw they were not alone. Sharing the car with them were a family of Hrund and two Grenlix. The Hrund smiled warmly and nodded, whilst the

Grenlix made a point of looking anywhere other than at the two warriors. Claire moved and sat next to Evie.

'What line is this?' she asked. 'I don't recognise half the station names, and the ones I do know are all from different lines.'

'It's like I said, this place is close enough to the Real to get you confident enough to make a stupid mistake. Just because something seems familiar, it usually isn't.'

They went four stops before Evie stood. Claire recognised the names of Aldgate and Whitechapel, but 'Commercial Road' rang no bells, and neither did 'Turner's Road', which was where they got off. The station wasn't deep and they were on the pavement after a single flight of stairs.

As soon as they came out onto the street, Claire felt a difference. The area around Tower Hill had been busy, but cosmopolitan. Here, just about everybody she could see was a Grenlick. Carts were being towed along with steam tractors, or by 'Grenlick-power', and everything looked worn and suffering from long use; paint peeled and repairs were frequent and obvious. An omnibus clattered arduously up the road and made hissing toots at children playing a game of chicken in front of it.

'Nice place,' said Claire, feeling nervous and doing her best not to show it. 'Where are we?'

'Doesn't have an official name,' Evie replied. 'It's sort of halfway between Poplar and Stepney, or would be in the Real. If the Grenlix have a name for it, nobody ever told me. Everybody calls it Turner's Road.'

They crossed over and started to walk down Cotton Street. It was quieter here, but there was still a hustle of commerce back and forth. It was the buildings that Claire found unsettled her most. There were no houses, only huge structures that looked like factories. They were all three floors tall, but along the ground floor of each were alcoves like railway arches, rather than windows. Some were bricked or boarded up, sometimes with small, unwelcoming doors. Most were open fronted shops with shutters folded out of the way on either side.

'Are these factories?' Claire asked, looking at the ranked windows above her.

Evie chuckled, the most relaxed sound she had made all day. 'No, that's a Hive. It's what Grenlix call the places they live. I suppose you could say it was like a block of flats, only they go down even farther then they go up.'

'Basements?'

Evie shrugged. 'I don't know much more. Grenlix don't give out info willingly, especially not about themselves. I think it's something to do with status, but whether up or down is good I wouldn't know. We need to go in here.'

They had stopped outside one of the alcoves. It had a more conventional shop front with a door and a display window, but the door was closed and the window was so coated with grime it was impossible to see inside. Everything was slightly scaled down and the door was barely big enough for her to walk through without stooping. Evie tried the handle but the door wouldn't budge. She raised a fist and hammered on it.

'Closed!' snarled a voice. 'Can't you read?'

Claire looked around the shop front but couldn't see any sign. Evie hammered on the door again.

'I said 'closed',' the voice said again. Evie put her lips close to the edge of the door and spoke, her voice not loud but intense. 'Get your ass over here and open this door or I'll start—'

Claire never found out what Evie was threatening to do because there was already a sound of bolts being drawn back and a key turning in a lock. The door swung open in to a gloomy interior, and she caught the outline of a diminutive, hunched body moving farther into the unlit depths of the shop. Evie gestured that she should step through, and when she hesitated gave her a shove. As soon as Claire moved inside she heard Evie shut the door behind them and throw one of the bolts.

The ceiling was only a couple of inches above her head, and her shoulders hunched no matter how much she told them the ceiling wasn't going to press down on them. The floor was littered with amorphous shapes concealed by dust sheets. They

75

reminded her uncomfortably of Morphs and she shivered.

There was a strange smell on the air, spicy yet musty and not entirely pleasant. It had an edge of mouldiness, and it caught at the back of Claire's mouth and made her want to cough. She was in the middle of turning to ask Evie what they were doing here and could she wait outside when a door at the far end of the room swung open and yellow light lifted the gloom slightly. Evie nudged her arm, and they walked towards the door.

The back room was all workbenches. Assorted unrecognisable devices littered the workbenches in various states of dismemberment and the place was instantly identifiable as somewhere things were mended. Two Grenlix sat on stools at the longest bench, studiously ignoring the humans. Claire guessed they were young, possibly apprentices. An older Grenlick stood in the middle of the room, obviously in charge and glaring suspiciously at her.

Claire decided this annoyed her. She had never done anything to this person, and he was judging her. She pulled herself up and set her shoulders back, pushing back the metaphysical weight of the ceiling, and looked coolly back at the proprietor. 'Greetings, Grenlick,' she said, tone even, and inclining her head.

To her surprise, some of the hardness went out of the Grenlick's expression, and she received a small bow in return. 'Greetings, Warrior.' The Grenlick turned its attention to Evie. 'What do you want, Jones?'

'You know what I want, to——,' she broke off and flicked a guilty look at Claire. 'You know what I want, Grenlick. Is it ready yet?'

Evie didn't get a straight answer. 'Who is she?' asked the Grenlick, jerking its head towards Claire.

'A new recruit. I'm training her.'

The Grenlick looked suspicious, but Evie didn't offer anything else. Eventually it turned back to Claire, and gave another little bow. 'Grenlick Krennet Tolks.'

'Warrior Claire Stone,' she responded, instinctively, and everybody in the room seemed to breathe out.

'So?' said Evie, and Claire thought she sounded like a ten year old at Christmas, hoping she had got the bike she wanted.

'It's ready,' Tolks admitted, with an air of reluctance. 'But it is not good, it is not proper.'

'But it does work?'

'Barely. The accuracy is... disappointing.'

'It will have to do. I've been waiting for months for one to turn up.'

Claire flicked her attention from one to the other like she was watching a game of tennis and didn't understand a word. There was a pause as Tolks seemed to be trying to find another argument, but its shoulders sagged in defeat.

'Very well, Jones. But I take no blame for this, and the device was not provided by me.'

Claire's eyebrows shot up and she tried to catch Evie's eye. It wasn't until Tolks turned and walked away through another door that Evie looked back.

'He's the best,' she said. 'Anything you need, or anything you need fixing, Tolks can find it or mend it.'

'So what's he doing for you?'

Evie's eyes slid away from Claire's. 'Oh, just a gadget I've been trying to find.'

'And this is honest? On the level? Nobody says 'you didn't get it from me' unless there's something hooky about it.'

Evie laughed, but it sounded fake. 'That's because he's not happy with the accuracy, not because it's bent.'

Claire let it lie. She didn't believe Evie but she had made her point, and though Evie hadn't outright lied, she still hadn't been open. In itself, that told Claire something. Tolks reappeared, carrying something wrapped in a cloth which he handed to Evie. Without unwrapping it, she tucked it away in a pocket before shaking hands with the Grenlick.

And that was it. No small talk, no leave taking. The Grenlick simply turned his back on them and walked away, and Evie gave Claire a gentle push back towards the door.

TEN

The next time Claire opened her locker she found that still more new toys had been deposited while she had been away, not the least of which was a weapon identical to the one she had used to rescue Evie, complete with a holster. A series of clips had been fixed to the back wall of the locker, and all she had to do was grab hold of it and pull.

'Do they always dig around in our lockers like this?' Claire asked.

Evie shrugged. 'Stores are handled by Grenlix. You couldn't keep them out if you tried.'

'But it's not very private.'

'Would you leave anything valuable or secret in your school locker?'

'No. Well, not for long.'

'Exactly. Besides, Grenlix have this weird honour thing. They'd never steal from us because they work for us, and they'd never open your locker without the right paperwork.' She paused and looked thoughtful. 'Of course, if they didn't work for us... Anyway, want to try it out?'

Claire nodded, resolving never to leave anything embarrassing in her locker.

Evie took them down into the basement again, and Claire found herself in a large space, big enough for three or four tennis courts. There were rails crisscrossed all over the ceiling, and in the corner a small steam engine hissed softly to itself. The area around the entrance was well lit, but the rest of the space was divided into pools of light, apparently deliberately. Evie stood in front of Claire and held her own weapon up in her hand.

'This is your basic Mk 22 Anti Incursion Weapon. It has an uprated absorption chamber for faster recharging in weak magical fields, and projects a cloud of fléchettes with an imbued property of being able to disrupt the surface tension of Morphs. We call it a PPG'

'A what?'

Evie grinned. 'Purple Puff Gun.'

She turned a valve on the engine in the corner and it began to chug with greater enthusiasm, its little foot long piston spinning a flywheel on a shaft that disappeared into the wall. Targets hanging on metal rods began to scoot around the tracks on the ceiling. There were thin sheets like cardboard that had targets painted on them, thicker sheets in the shapes of Morphs and Hrund and Angels, and things that looked like punching bags.

Evie started Claire off aiming at the small targets. A hit glowed briefly for few seconds then faded away, and on the far wall two counters kept score. Evie went into the lead straight away, and scored twenty first. A harsh buzzer sounded a moment and everything stopped moving. Claire had only scored twelve and was not pleased.

'Level 2?' Evie asked. Claire had no idea what 'level 2' entailed, but she shrugged agreement anyway. Evie fiddled with something by the engine and the targets all repositioned themselves. Two Morph-shapes positioned themselves at the front of the two girls and the counters both counted down from five. At the last instant Evie said 'Catch it if you can' and she ran off after her target, which had shot off down the hall

The target in front of Claire also moved. Claire ran after it, bringing her PPG up for a running shot. A split second later one of the punch bags knocked her from her feet and sent her rolling across the floor. Claire sat up, furious at Evie for not warning her, but then the intricacies of what the game was doing caught her curiosity. Padded bags tried to knock her over, other targets kept blocking her line of sight, and if she stayed still too long something would tag her.

She looked up at her scoreboard. Minus 10! Already! A cardboard Grenlick zoomed towards her and she rolled out of its way, coming to her feet as part of the same motion. Another quick look around and she spotted her target near the far end of the room. She started to trot towards it, zapped a Morph coming in from her left, and dodged a smiling Hrund lady with a child.

She took two more incidental hits on passing Morphs, then managed a hit on her personal nemesis. She flicked a look up to the scoreboard. She was almost level with Evie. Her grin got tighter and her eyes narrowed. This was fun.

Claire had no idea how much time had passed when the buzzer sounded to mark the end of the level, and had even less sense of what her score might be. She had been bowled over again, but had seen Evie rolling across the floor at least twice, so didn't feel so bad. See looked around, found Evie, and walked over to her. Evie was breathing hard and didn't look happy. Claire's, with a slightly sick feeling, wondered just what had to happen to keep the girl smiling.

'How did we do?' Claire asked, trying to keep her voice as neutral as she could. Evie said nothing, but jabbed her chin in the general direction of the board. Claire turned, and felt her mouth hang open. It had to be a mistake. There was more information than before, but it looked like she had beaten Evie. Only by two marks, but that would be enough to explain the foul expression on Evie's face.

There was one pair of numbers, coloured red, where Evie had scored more than Claire, so she figured she had to be safe talking about those. 'What are the red ones? You got a fair few more of them than me.'

Evie turned to face her and positively glared. 'Shooting the wrong target,' she said in an icy voice, and walked over to fiddle with the engine. When Claire wandered over, Evie suddenly turned on her. 'What's the time?'

'I... uh...' Claire didn't have a clue. Not even close. She raised her arm to look at her watch, but it wasn't there and that was the moment she remembered she had decided not to wear it in case it got scratched. Her parents had bought it for her last Christmas, and she really liked it. 'What time was it when you jumped in?' 'I don't know that either,' she replied.

'You have to. You always need to be aware how long you have been down here. What if you had stayed over your Snapback time? It could be midnight in the real and the only place you can jump out to is the library, and that's closed.' 'What?' said Claire, panicking. Her parents would be worrying, and after the disaster with the 'Bleeding Black Hearts' episode, she really didn't...

'Relax. I said 'what if'. You still have time to snap back.'

'Then why did you say it?' said Claire, trying not to get mad. 'That scared me.'

'It was meant to. I wanted you to think about what might have happened.'

Claire looked at her PPG for a moment, trying to push aside the image of her shooting it at Evie, then very carefully made sure the safety was on before slipping it back into its holster. 'Why not show me a 'snap back' and we can call it a day.'

Evie, unapologetic, looked her in the eyes for a moment before turning away. They said nothing on the walk back to the locker room, or while each of them stored their gear away. When Evie came to stand next to her, Claire felt herself stiffen.

'It's not much of a difference,' Evie explained. 'But you have to think of when you are going as much as where. You didn't check the time, so you can't practise, but you can watch me.'

Evie took her arms and Claire felt the peculiar turn in and direction that wasn't really there, but this time there was an extra pull that she hadn't felt before, and then they were back in the archives of the library. Evie let go and stepped away as soon as they were balanced, and seemed to be waiting for something.

'Aren't you going back?' Claire asked.

'Can't. We snapped back two hours and five minutes. I can't jump back in for that long.'

Claire was about to ask why when she saw the problem herself. 'Or you would be there twice?' Evie nodded. 'Suppose we better leave the hard way, then.'

They walked out into the mid afternoon sunshine. Around them, the shopping complex was moderately busy but not manic and Claire decided she needed to do something about her thirst. 'Fancy a smoothie or something,' she offered, wondering if Evie would accept and not sure if she really wanted her to or not.

Evie shrugged. 'Why not.'

Claire took them to a milkshake bar where you could get the most astonishing range of utterly bizarre things turned into milkshakes. She selected a fairly mundane double-banana, but after several minutes of agonising over three different types of candy, Evie plumped for something involving a chocolate crème egg and a honeycomb bar. Even the machine operator looked impressed by the combination, although it left Claire wondering about the rest of Evie's diet. They took seats at small metal tables outside the shop and watched the world go by.

The silence felt awkward and Evie didn't seem about to chat, so Claire decided to try and kick-start something. 'I just realised you could be from anywhere,' she said.

Evie finished a long and, by the way the straw caved in quite difficult, pull from her drink and savoured it for a moment before answering.

'Yup.'

Claire tried again. 'But you must live pretty close. I mean, your accent is London-ish. Not that I'm any good at that sort of thing.'

'No, close enough. Around Harland.'

That was about ten miles north; a medium sized 'new town' with an undistinguished reputation. Not bad, or nasty, but not nice either. Claire gritted her teeth, thought about blood and stones, and tried one more time.

'What does your dad do?'

Evie stopped in mid suck and her lips unglued from around the straw with a soft 'pop'. She lifted her head and stared straight into Claire's eyes. Claire dropped her head. The contact was too intense.

'What's with the twenty questions routine?'

'Sorry. I was just chatting.'

'You were poking.'

'All right, maybe I was,' Claire admitted, feeling her face flush. 'I don't know anything about you. You know where I live, what my mum does. Loads.'

Evie stared at her a little longer. Her eyes were still piercing, but some of the hostility had faded. Abruptly she looked away and took another drag on her viscous milkshake.

'My dad left us when I was three, or so my mum said. She didn't take it too well, and by the time I was eight I was in care. Still can't get a straight answer if they took me or she gave me up. Been there ever since. Still there. Expect they'll kick me out in a year or so. As soon as I finish sixth form at college anyway. That enough?'

Claire mumbled something that sounded something like 'sorry' and began to wonder if she could make an excuse, dump the remaining half of her milkshake and leave. It seemed too rude, somehow. On the other hand, if she tried to drink the milkshake any faster, she would get brain freeze. She was starting to rummage around in her pockets, getting ready to check for mobile and return ticket, when Evie let out a deep sigh.

'I'm sorry. I'm not good with people, so I always think that someone asking questions is after something. My mum left me long before I went into care. Years before. I thought it was because of my dad. She seemed to turn in on herself and away from me, and I thought she couldn't handle being on her own, or that it was my fault, or all the usual bullshit the trick cyclists try to make you think of when they 'analyse' you. So they took me

84

into care, and only a couple of weeks later someone recruited me, and it was then I realised. My mum had been infected by a Morph.'

Claire felt her eyebrows shoot up even though she tried to stop them, and she bit down on her tongue to stop herself speaking. Her instinct was to argue, or to at least suggest there were an awful lot of other answers, but there was a look on Evie's face that told her that would be a waste of time. It was the look she had seen on the faces of evangelists when she had been studying 'World Religions'.

'So I knew I had to do everything I could to help in Underland, and to be the best Warrior they had ever had. Maybe one day even find a way to get the Morphs out of people in the Real.'

'Do you still see your mum?'

Evie shook her head. 'She's not interested, but Smeggie Knicks says they have an address for her when I'm ready for it.'

'Who?'

Evie giggled, the first happy sound Claire had heard from her since the PPG practise. 'Meg Nixon, our shelter supervisor. We all call her 'Smeggie Knicks'. She's all right, though.' She drew on the straw again and was rewarded only with an intestinal gurgle. 'Finished. As am I. See you later.'

'Where? When? Tomorrow?'

Evie thought for a moment. 'No. You'll be tired later today. Try to stay up until your normal bed time, though. You'll probably be tired tomorrow too. Monday. Same place. Ten o'clock.'

Claire nodded and, with a nonchalant wave, Evie strode off.

ELEVEN

'How much trouble am I in?' Claire asked as they walked along Lower Thames Street. It was early evening, and the neutral yellow sky was fading towards ochre. For the last two weeks, Claire had met Evie every other day. Tracking, target practice, and traipsing around the simulacrum of central London had taken the majority of the training time. That, and practising jumps. Even though Evie swore she could feel Claire pulling away from her, Claire still could not make her own way in or out.

'None,' Evie said, turning her head to smile. 'Some take to it easier than others. I told you.'

'But the ones that can't do it. How are they weeded out?'

'Used to be if they couldn't jump in on their own that was as far as they got, then they relaxed it so that you could get help jumping in, but you had to jump out on your own. Eventually.'

'How long is 'eventually'?'

Evie stopped and turned to face her. 'Look, stop obsessing about it. It's like most things, the more you let yourself stress out the more difficult it gets. We've been given three months to train you. You've only used two weeks.'

'But it's not usual. To take this long, I mean.'

Evie growled, threw up her arms and walked off. Claire had to jog for a few steps to catch up. She wasn't surprised. Evie had been getting easier to upset for the past week, and half the time seemed to be lost in a world of her own. Claire had started to wonder if the training was more than Evie had bargained for, but decided to let the matter drop. Maybe Evie was right, and the best thing to do was try to ignore it. She poked Evie in the arm as she drew level.

'Where are we going?'

'Observer Station,' Evie replied.

'Is it far?'

Evie pointed ahead of them. A slender tower sprouted from the top of a tall building about four hundred metres away. Claire squashed a groan. Heights weren't her thing.

The building was anonymous. There were no signs or names over the letterboxes, and the door wasn't locked. To Claire's delight there was an old fashioned elevator. She insisted on pulling the old-style metal grilles across herself, and on working the lever to make it go up. It wheezed and rattled so alarmingly that she decided to take the stairs back down when it was time to leave.

The carpet along the top floor corridor was worn to the weft and the woodwork had an air of neglect. Evie led them to the far end and opened a door without knocking. Behind was a very mundane office, staffed by teenagers. Everybody in the room looked up in surprise as they entered. Most turned back to what they were doing, but a few stared; a mixture of expressions ranging from awed to disdainful. In one corner a Warrior sprawled on a couch. He nodded politely to them, but also made no attempt to hide his interest.

A fussy looking girl, who looked a year or so younger than Claire and instantly reminded her of Melanie Styke, rose from a desk and started to walk across the room. 'Warriors are not supposed to be here unless it's their duty post.'

Claire felt Evie bristle beside her, like a sudden static field making the hairs on her arm prickle, and she found herself largely agreeing. 'Familiarization visit,' said Evie, voice tight and terse.

'We weren't notified, so you'll have to—'

A door to the left opened and a young man walked across the room. 'I'll deal with this, Sooz.'

'But they're supposed to —'

'I said I'll handle it.' It was the boy from the locker room, and Claire struggled to remember his name. He looked pointedly at Sooz and raised his eyebrows. Sooz held her position for a moment longer then stomped back to the desk she had been sitting at.

'Sorry about that,' said Jack Cooper. 'Can I help you?'

Claire saw he was looking at her, not at Evie, and she felt her cheeks start to glow. His hair looked different to how she remembered; spikier, as though he had gelled it. It looked better.

'Like I said, I wanted to show her an Observation post.' Evie's voice still had an edge, but she sounded less hostile.

'Sure,' said Jack. 'Want the full tour?' He was still looking at Claire, not Evie.

Claire glanced as Evie to see how she should answer, but Evie seemed to be thinking about something else.

'Tell you what, Jones-'

Evie's attention suddenly snapped back to the now. 'That's *Warrior* Jones.'

Jack's eyes started to roll, but he stopped them. 'Sorry. *Warrior* Jones. Anyway, what I was going to say was would you like to leave Warrior…?'

'Stone,' Claire supplied.

'With me for a couple of hours? I can give her the tour, explain the procedures, and so on.'

'Yeah. OK.'

Claire almost gave herself whiplash turning her head to look at Evie, and she felt her mouth hanging open.

'I have something I need to do for a bit, and you'd only be bored,' Evie explained, but she didn't look Claire in the eyes as she spoke. 'If Cooper doesn't mind you getting under his feet for a couple of hours, it might be a good idea.'

'Not at all,' said Jack, a little too quickly, and Claire turned back to him with her eyes narrowed. As soon as she looked away, Evie turned and walked out of the room, throwing a 'see you' over her shoulder as the door closed behind her. Claire became uncomfortably aware that most of the eyes in the room were on her again.

'So, ah, what goes on at an observation post?' she asked, then winced as she realised how lame she sounded.

'If you did things right, you'd know,' muttered a voice behind her, then she jumped as Jack barked 'Enough,' glaring at someone over her shoulder before inviting Claire over to the other side of the room with a gesture. Tucked into a corner was a battered desk, with a chair either side and a pile of papers at one end. At the other end were two mugs, one of which looked like it had been there for a while, a baggie with half a sandwich in it, and a battered copy of 'Friday' by Robert Heinlein lying open and spine up. Behind and slightly to the side of the desk was a huge map that covered most of the wall. Claire walked up to it and peered closely. It was exquisitely detailed and, so far as she could tell, hand drawn.

'Beautiful, isn't it?' said Jack. Claire jumped. He was standing right next to her and she had forgotten he was there. She took the seat on the far side of the desk, and Jack began to tell her about the day-to-day workings of an Observation Post.

It wasn't that he was a boring speaker. His voice didn't have that horrible jobsworth drone like teachers dragging their way one term closer to their retirement, but the material was not inspiring. Rotas, maximum watch times, certifications, warrior locations, use of runners depending on age and enough detail to make her eyes glaze over after twenty minutes. She tried so hard to look interested, fidgeting from side to side, pushing a fingernail into the cuticle of her thumb. Every last trick of the bored student trying hard not to nod off, and all ultimately of no use when she realised Jack had stopped talking and was looking at her with a crooked smile.

90

'It is a bit much to take in all at once,' he said.

Claire nodded, afraid her boredom had been too obvious and she had offended him, but Jack looked bright enough and was smiling.

'How about we go and see where it's all done?'

'On the roof?'

'Up the tower.'

'I don't know. I'm not that good with heights.'

'Perfectly safe. Trust me?'

'No,' Claire replied, but smiled.

Jack led her to another door in the room. 'Up top if anybody wants me,' he said to the room, and there was a muted mutter of acknowledgement as he opened the door and invited Claire to climb the flight of stairs on the other side.

The roof was flat and had a low brick wall around it. Claire thought they were quite high enough, and that the wall looked totally inadequate. The view was expansive. To the east she could see the Tower of London, and to the west Mount Primrose dominated the skyline. Then she turned around and saw the wooden observation tower. She wasn't sure how tall it was, but it was too tall. With ladders leading up inside, it looked entirely too narrow to support the platform at the top.

'I am *not* going up that.'

'It really is safe,' said Jack, putting what Claire assumed he thought looked like an encouraging smile.

'I don't think I care.'

Jack chuckled, but instead of trying to persuade her further he turned to the tower and shouted up at it, hands cupped around his mouth. 'O'Malley. Drop something. Something big.'

There was a brief pause then a silhouette marred the straight lines of the platform's edge. A moment later something was thrown outwards from the platform. It looked about the size of a child's head, and it was falling very quickly. Claire was drawing in breath to squeal and was shifting her weight ready to step back when whatever it was started to slow, drifting gently inwards towards the tower. It came to a gentle halt on the roof, right at the foot of the first ladder. 'Safety net,' said Jack, grinning. 'Every tower has one. Magical, obviously. Now, sure you won't come up?' He picked up the bag and hooked an arm through it. 'I have to take this back up or O'Malley will moan for days. Honestly, you have to see it to believe it.'

Claire desperately wanted to say 'no', but this was about saving face. She was supposed to be a Warrior, and a she didn't want to be known as the one who wouldn't go up the tower. She clenched her jaw and nodded. Jack beamed a smile and stood back. 'You first, then I can help if you need anything.'

Claire reached out with shaking hands, and took hold of the rung in front of her eyes. Liquid tingles ran down the back of her legs and her heart started to hammer uncomfortably in her ears.

She stared intently at the ladder, refusing to look beyond it or, worse, down, and started to climb. She started counting, but somewhere around twenty the numbers slipped away as she concentrated on the sequence hand-hand-foot, gripping so hard that she was surprised she didn't leave dents in the wood.

Eventually, she sensed the looming bulk of the platform in her peripheral vision, and then the floor was passing in front of her. Helpful hands reached down to haul her the last few feet, and she got an impromptu round of applause. Jack clattered up behind her, and the trap door slammed shut.

'Well done,' he said. 'Not everybody can make it up here, and few Warriors ever bother. People will talk about you.'

'I think they already are,' said Claire, earning her a chuckle from all three observers. Apart from Jack, there was a girl of around twelve, and a boy perhaps a year older. Both were wearing goggles, but of a subtly different design to hers. They were bigger, with wider lenses that had thick wires coiled around their edges, like the coils on her Kevlar amulet. They stood at the edge of the platform and scanned their heads from side to side like radar dishes.

'Want to see our world?' Jack asked, holding out a pair of goggles.

TWELVE

Claire hesitated for a heartbeat before taking the goggles from Jack's hand. As she put them up to her eyes she caught a hint of citrus and the seaside, and guessed they were Jack's own. She approved of his taste in aftershave, not that he looked like the shaving part was too much of a problem yet.

As the goggles settled over her eyes everything went black exactly as it did with her own, and again there was the ripple of shifting colour as the lenses cleared. This time, though, the view was very dark, almost black, and she didn't feel she could see enough to move.

'Let me help,' Jack said, softly and too close to her ear. A little shiver tickled between her shoulder blades that she was almost certain was due to being in the dark atop the tower. Almost. 'They can be a bit scary the first time you put them on.' She felt him take a gentle hold of her arm and he led her forwards.

Claire felt the top of the wall around the platform press against her, just below the ribs, then gasped. 'Oh, wow.'

Under-London spread out beneath her in a mesh of soft, dark blue, sparkling like Tinkerbell's contrail. Lighter local hotspots were scattered here and there, but the structure of London was reduced to silhouettes against an ultramarine background. Tiny streaks of bright scarlet like individual raindrops of fire shot downwards at random intervals. 'What are you looking for?' she asked.

'Incursions,' said Jack. 'If you're really good, you can see a change in the background a few seconds before, but most of the time we only see when an incursion is in progress. Then you know it. It's like a pillar of fire, white or yellow, shooting up from the ground. The trick is in figuring out where it's coming from when all you have is shadows of buildings.'

'And the little red sparks?'

There was a pause. 'Pardon?'

'The little red sparks coming down?'

There was a slightly longer silence than there should have been, and Jack's voice didn't sound quite right as he gently turned Claire away from the rail. 'Perhaps that's enough for now. These goggles can take some getting used to. The sparks are probably just your eyes adjusting to the magic, or the other way around.'

Claire heard a lie in his voice. Not a very big one, and more about protecting her than hiding something. The door on the roof opened, distracting them both and taking away her opportunity to dig deeper. Voices were followed by the crunch of feet on the gravel of the roof, then the clatter of feet on the ladder. The two observers already on the platform removed their goggles, waved, and jumped over the edge. Claire squealed, then remembered the magical safety net and felt stupid.

'It's quicker,' Jack explained. 'This platform is only rated for four people. And I suppose maybe a bit of showing off for the visitor. Officially, I should be grumpy about it, but it doesn't hurt anyone.'

The two new observers took up posts with barely a nod to her or Jack, and she realised they were in the way. It was an utterly impressive sight, but one that she had seen enough of and there was still the problem of getting down again.

It took a while, but Claire eventually managed to get her feet back down to the roof. Conflicting feelings of being on something much firmer, but still way too high, left her slightly dizzy until they went back down the stairs to the office. Evie hadn't returned, and they were in that awkward place where Claire really should have left but couldn't.

'So, has Warrior Jones shown you about much,' Jack asked as they sat at his desk.

Claire nodded, then twisted her lips to one side. 'Sort of. We've done a lot of tracking old incursions. That's got us around a bit.'

'But all business?'

Claire nodded.

'That sounds like Jones,' said Jack, with a wry smile, then an idea seemed to occur to him. Whatever it was, she could see the indecision on his face. 'Look, I'm due off shift now anyway. How would you like to go and see a couple of the real sights, not work stuff?'

'I don't think so,' Claire replied slowly. Jack's face fell and he looked embarrassed. 'Not because it doesn't sound interesting, but–' and it was her turn to hesitate. This was not an admission she wanted to make in public, but Jack had been very kind and she owed him the truth. She leaned forward across the desk, and he did the same. 'I can't jump in or out on my own yet. Evie, I mean 'Warrior Jones', picks me up and drops me back.'

Jack sat back in his chair with an 'Ah' of understanding. 'Awkward.' He mused for a minute, and a smile gradually climbed up his face. 'Sod her. She wandered off to do something else and didn't say when she'd be back. Let's bunk off for a couple of hours. She can either wait here or leave a message where to meet her.'

Claire thought about how pissy Evie could get, and how likely it was this would set her off, and she thought about how Jack was right and things had been very much work and very little play. She made up her mind, and returned a matching grin.

'Why not.'

Fifteen minutes later they were on the street and heading for the nearest underground station. 'I don't know if this is the sort of thing that will get to you,' Jack explained. 'It certainly got to me, and if it doesn't float your boat it'll give me a better idea of the things you do like.' Beyond that, he would offer nothing more in explanation, and exacted a promise that she would do what he said no matter how weird it got. Claire had to think hard about that one. There were stories about people who asked for commitments like that, but Jack didn't seem the type, and all she was doing was promising. She could still bail if anything started to get too uncomfortable.

They got off at a station called 'Broad Street'. Again, not one that Claire recognised, but there was something she thought she ought to remember about the name. As soon as they got off the train, Jack asked her to keep her eyes on the ground. It was a surface level station, so there weren't many steps, but when they were in the ticket hall, Jack upped the stakes.

'I want you to shut your eyes and let me lead you. One flight of stairs and a dozen paces either end.'

Claire hesitated for a second. They were in a public place. There were Grenlix and Sathaari and Hrund all around them. What could go wrong? She nodded, closed her eyes and felt his hand take her arm. She didn't actually count the steps, but he had been close. At the bottom of the stairs the sound dynamics changed suddenly from an enclosed space to something cavernous.

'Look straight ahead, and open your eyes,' said Jack.

Her eyes opened, and kept going, while her mouth opened in a soundless gasp. She didn't know where to look, overwhelmed by the sheer number of things to see. The space they were in was beyond vast, and could have accommodated a couple of cathedrals. Astonishing enough under normal circumstances, but directly in front of her was an airship. Beside it, another. The gasbags looked to be the size of blue whales, and there was a gondola hanging beneath bigger than a train carriage.

Somewhere a whistle sounded; not a little 'toot toot' but a resounding blast that said it meant business and that something important was about to happen. Jack tapped her on the shoulder and pointed at a space on the roof, farther back than the two airships and off to the left.

The whistle sounded again, and was followed by a screech as some enormous clutch engaged. Far above there was a loud, metallic 'thunk' followed by the grinding of gears. A cracked formed in the roof, and Claire realised that a pair of enormous shutters were folding open.

With another thump the doors stopped moving, and the whistle gave two short blasts. From behind the two airships blocking her view, Claire heard huge great propellers start to beat and, with ponderous grace, a behemoth eased itself into the air. At first, Claire thought two airships were rising at the same time, but then she realised they were bound together. Tail surfaces flapped up and down, back and forth, as though they were undergoing one last check. Then the bottom of the gasbags came into view. Beneath each was a gondola, easily four times the size of the ones before her. Three engine pods stuck out from either side, fully steerable, and were currently pointing downwards to ease the monster into the air. As it passed through the roof, there was the slightest ripple in the outer skin as the wind stroked against it, showing the outline of the ribs beneath . An even deeper thrum beat down into the cavernous hanger, and as the airship moved off Claire could see the three gargantuan primary rotors at the rear of the vessel beating the air to drive the airship forward.

'Daily shuttle to Petit Paris,' said Jack, just loud enough to be heard. 'I thought we might be in time to see her go.'

Claire nodded, awestruck, still looking up as the roof doors rumbled closed.

'You like?' Jack asked. Claire nodded again, still speechless. 'My kind of geek,' he said with a satisfied nod.

The two hours they had allotted themselves passed in minutes of subjective time, and their excursion went no further than

97

Broad Street Terminus. When Claire satiated herself on airships, there were the rail platforms along which steam trains pulled freight and passenger cars out to who knew where. A brief break for a squash, and it was time to head back to the Observation station at the corner of Eastcheap and Philpot lane. At the front door, Claire caught Jack's arm and pulled him to one side. 'I need a favour.'

'If I can.'

'If this works, can you tell Evie – I mean Warrior Jones – usual place and time, day after tomorrow.' She took her PPG from its holster and handed it to him.

Jack took the weapon like she had handed him a dead rat, but checked the safety with an automatic movement and a casual competence that made Claire do a double-take. 'Why, what are you–'

Claire had already taken two steps back from Jack, smiling at him, and was pulling in her will, focusing her thoughts on the stacks of the archives, thinking of herself looking at her watch at 10:22. There was no Evie, no pressure. Nothing to stop her except herself. She held all this inside, drew in a breath to go with it, and turned directly into a high table holding back issues of the Hertfordshire Mercury. She put out her hands to steady herself, and started to laugh.

THIRTEEN

Two days later Claire tried the same trick to jump in, only this time focusing on the front of her locker. She was already wearing her warrior gear. It even had the approval of her parents, impressed with her 'new look' and the offer of a shopping trip to buy some really imposing boots from her mother. Nothing happened. When she had jumped out there had been a sense of anticipation, but this morning she could feel nothing except tension. She sighed, picked up her student pass, and started walking to the bus stop.

Evie was, as usual, late and jumped into the archives so close to Claire that she felt the displacement pushing her away a moment before Evie arrived. Evie just looked at her for a moment, expression indecipherable apart from a slight frown, then she lightly pursed her lips and shrugged.

'Think you can do it again?'

'Don't know.'

'If you can, one rule. Apart from your Kevlar, never, ever, take any Underland technology out into the Real.'

'OK' Claire didn't mention the phone in her pocket, or the torch or the goggles.

'Come on then.'

'I still can't jump in. I already tried today.'

Evie took her arms and jumped them into the locker room. 'Now, can you jump out again?'

Claire tried, but it was like when she had been at home. She felt nothing except tension. She felt her eyes start to fill. 'I'm never going to get the hang of this,' she wailed.

Evie said nothing, and when Claire glanced at her she looked horribly embarrassed. Claire hoped it wasn't because of her weeping. 'You know it could be me,' said Evie. 'I could be putting you off, making you nervous.'

Claire sniffed. The thought had crossed her mind, but she had been too unsure of herself to suggest it. Evie was so confident, so imposing, that Claire sometimes felt it was inevitable she would never measure up. She nodded. 'Might be.'

Claire saw a shadow of disappointment, and possibly hurt, on Evie's face, and there was an uncharacteristic slump to her shoulders. She felt bad. She hadn't meant to hurt Evie.

'No,' Evie pulled herself up. 'The more I think of it the more I think it might be a good idea. Give you a different perspective on things. There must be another Warrior I can ask.' The last came out quieter, slower, as if she wasn't sure there was.

'Or an observer?' said Claire, then she felt her cheeks get hot at the very direct look Evie gave her. 'I only meant that another warrior would be just as intimidating,' she added, knowing that no matter what she said it would sound lame.'

'Let's think about it,' said Evie. 'For now, target practice then tracking.'

Claire groaned.

They called a halt by mutual consent six hours later. Evie had allowed them one short break, but otherwise they had been busy the whole time and Claire was tired. They had just walked into the locker room, when something buzzed in her pocket, and there was a chirping noise.

'Are you going to answer that?' asked Evie, looking intrigued.

'Answer what?' said Claire, then she remembered the Underland phone she carried. So far, she hadn't has reason to use it. Now, it seemed someone was calling her. She took it out of her pocket. 'Hello?' It tingled in her hand as it made the connection.

'Claire? It's Jack. Jack Cooper? I remembered you said you might be in Underland today. Wondered if you knew what time you were finishing?'

Claire turned away from Evie's arch look, face flaming and wishing the call was more private. 'Why?'

Jack's voice lost all its confidence. 'Well, I thought you might like to spend an hour or two looking around the place some more. Maybe doing some map work and going through some of the major differences between Underland and the Real.'

Claire turned back to Evie and raised her eyebrows. Evie frowned, then snapped 'Whatever' before turning and marching out of the locker room. Claire's eyebrows climbed higher, and she was torn between chasing after Evie to see what the matter was and letting her stomp off and get whatever it was out of her system. She must have thought about it longer than she realised.

'Claire?' Jack's voice sounded concerned now. 'Is everything OK?'

'Sounds good to me. Where are you?'

Stepping onto the streets of Underland was a very different feeling when she was on her own. She still wore her 'uniform', her PPG holstered along her leg, but she felt a total fraud. As she walked up to the Lower Thames Street checkpoint the two guards – both Hrund – watched her impassively. She saw judgement in their eyes and she unconsciously slowed down, her confidence evaporating by the second. Where there was only mild curiosity she saw scorn and amusement. She stopped, ready to turn and run back to the locker room.

One of the Hrund stepped forward, stood to attention in front of her and gave a sharp bow. 'Warrior, is there something I can do for you? You seem… distracted.'

Claire nodded politely back, but what was she to do? The Hrund was looking at her, expecting an answer. But he had called her Warrior, and saluted her. She stood up straight.

'Thank you, Ser. I was deep in thought. I'm grateful for your concern.'

The Hrund smiled, gave her another bow, and returned to his post. Claire gave him enough time so it didn't look like she was following him and walked towards the gate herself. In a moment was out onto the street.

She knocked on the door to the observation post before she opened it and walked into chaos. Jack, the sour girl, and a Warrior were clustered around the map while a younger observer, looking very pale and shocked, sat in Jack's chair answering questions.. 'Is this a bad time?'

'We've got an incursion,' Jack threw over his shoulder at the same moment as the sour girl glared at her. 'Give me a minute.'

There were more hurried questions, a brief argument over a specific point on the map, and the Warrior strode purposefully towards the door. He patted his Kevlar and his PPG before he covered his eyes with his goggles. The door slammed behind him and the room was silent.

People eventually returned to whatever they were doing. Jack sat at his desk, running a hand up through his already dishevelled hair. 'Sorry about that.'

'No problem. Want to leave it for today?'

Jack's pursed his lips and puffed air. 'No, don't think so. In fact, want to go through the process?'

'Sure.' Claire accepted the offer more enthusiastically than she expected, and she wasn't sure why she was so pleased Jack hadn't taken her up on her offer to bail. He went through how the observer who made the visual would hammer down the stairs to the office, then they would discuss where on the map the incursion flare probably was, then the duty warrior would head out to find the trail and follow it.

'So your Warrior is already out, what happens then?'

'Runners. One to the nearest observation post, one to the

102

office. And we put our flag up to say we are dealing with an incident.'

It was Claire's turn to frown. 'That's got so many holes in it,' she complained. 'How often does it go wrong?'

Jack pulled a face. 'More often than I like, and way more than we admit. Are you OK?'

Claire felt something in her head. It felt like a pulse of something making her mind stretch like a sigh, and for a moment she was dizzy. It passed in seconds and she put up a hand to stop Jack, who was already halfway around the desk with his hands out to catch her. He still took her arm, and she had to admit it felt nice and grounded her.

'I'm fine–' was as far as she got before there was the sound of running feet outside the door. Somebody was shouting, and Jack's face went pale. 'Another one?' she asked, and all Jack could do was shrug.

She was pushed aside as another observer joined Jack and a new huddle formed around the map. She noticed, amid all the fuss, a quiet looking girl of no more than twelve pick up her coat and head out, presumably to make sure there was enough coverage on the platform.

'It was right on top of us,'

'Be specific.'

'I mean it. I saw it on the ground. Right at the end of Eastcheap. It headed south.'

'Shit. It could be heading for the river, or for one of the docks. Send runners to the Tower. Who else is available?' asked Jack

'St Swithins, Leadenhall and the Tower are all running flags. They may have sent out warriors against the last one.' 'A decoy?' asked the sour girl.

'Perhaps, but what the hell do we do now?'

Claire stood up and, in unconscious mimicry of the other warrior, touched her Kevlar and her PPG before taking her goggles out of her pocket.

'I'll go.'

FOURTEEN

'You can't,' said Jack. 'You're only a trainee.'

'I'm not going to try to *catch* it,' she replied, scornfully. 'I'm just going to track it and keep an eye on it until someone who knows what they're doing can get there. Otherwise it could get away, right?'

Jack nodded, reluctantly, and Claire walked purposefully out of the room.

Running was not something that she did unless she had to, but this seemed to be one of the occasions when it was required. After clattering down the stairs, she managed something between a trot and a run up Eastcheap, pulling her goggles on as she went, and not even slowing as she found the puddle of bright that marked the Morph's entry point. Through the clearer, top half of her goggles she could see that the slime had already dried away and had left no mark on the street.

The trail took her down Fish Street, then under the King William St bridge and onto Upper Thames Street. There were more people here, most huddled up against walls or in doorways, looking shocked or angry. The few that were on the street melted away in front of her, and one or two of the more helpful citizens pointed along the road in the direction the

Morph had travelled. She even heard a shout of encouragement.

The trail went under something that looked like it might be a railway station, then it ducked down towards the river, twisting and turning through one narrow alley after another. Claire jogged along as quickly as she could, but her breath started to burn in her chest and her throat started to close up. Exercise still wasn't her strong point.

The trail of the Morph turned south again and headed for the river. Claire began to worry. Someone had said it would head for the water, and it had sounded like this was a bad thing. Maybe they could still run underwater, or they morphed into a fish, or something. The silver trail led up to the end of the road, then disappeared. She slowed down, trying to catch her breath as she walked, expecting to look over the edge and see the river.

Only there was no water. It was low tide, and what she saw was a short flight of stone steps that led down to the riverbank. The smell was disgusting and she threw up a little into her mouth before she got herself under control. She spat unpleasantly, then looked down the steps and along the bank. Everything was a mess. The steps were coated in damp algae that looked as slippery as Morph slime, and the riverbank was cluttered with rubbish: discarded boxes, half-filled sacks and anonymous humps she really didn't want to know anything more about. All coated with a thick layer of river sludge.

Claire scanned back and forth, searching for a silver trail. There wasn't so much as a trace. She could see it going down the steps, but it got fainter the farther it went into the silt. She stamped her foot in frustration and punched her fists against her thighs. So close, and now she was going to be a joke. Nobody would take her seriously after this; the wannabe warrior who lost her first Morph.

She pulled her goggles away from her eyes and let them dangle around her neck. She had to blink a few times before her vision came back into focus. Losing the split-view of the goggles made her eyes water as they adjusted – or that was what she told herself. She wondered if she should head back to the

Tower. She could drop off her kit before she jumped home for the last time. She took one more look around as she turned, and froze in the middle of taking the first step.

There was a groove in the sludge. The side of her mouth hitched up into a lop-sided grin. The groove was shallow, and only six inches wide, but it clearly moved away from the steps and headed west along the riverbank. She picked her way gingerly down the steps and groaned as her boots sank two inches deep into the sludge.

When the groove finally faded out, Claire was standing close to a slipway. She put the goggles on, then punched the air and hissed 'Yessss' as a silver trail sprang to life in front of her. She jogged up the slipway, then followed the trail as it turned though a set of open gates. They were wooden, with patches of peeling paint and a sign above that said 'Queenshithe Wharf.'.

Claire hesitated at the entrance. The Morph could be trapped in there. Farther up the street there seemed to be some a commotion going on, but the trail definitely led into the wharf. A moment later, a Grenlick ran through the gates, eyes wide, pushing past her and looking anxiously over his shoulder. He pointed an unsteady finger back towards the gates and said 'It's in there' as he hurried off to join his companions at the end of the street.

She looked into the yard. Opposite her was what seemed to be a block of offices and to her right a larger structure with several barn-sized doors. From the back she guessed the buildings on either side of the gate might be the same. In the yard were piles of crates, laid out in a haphazard arrangement that rose higher than her head.

This had 'trap' written all over it. She could see the trail going through the gate, then turning left before it was hidden from view. The sensible thing to do was to stand at the gate and wait for help. She'd tracked it this far, and she couldn't see how it could get out. That was as much as anyone could reasonably ask of her. Except she wasn't sure. She couldn't see the whole yard. There could be another gate on the other side, and then she

107

would look exceptionally stupid for not checking.

Claire reached down and snapped the loop off the PPG's holster before carefully drawing the gun and giving it a quick visual check. The charge jewel said it was full, so she flicked off the safety and eased into the yard.

Pat of her wanted to take her goggles off, a primitive part of her brain that wanted to see everything it could without anything in the way, and if Claire could have guaranteed that the Morph would stay in monster shape, she would have taken the chance. But for all she knew it could be one of the larger crates. Nobody had told her what a Morph could change into. The only way she knew what she was looking at was the trail of silver that led to it.

The wall to her left looked clean; no boxes, only a blank wall with one double door. She put her back to it and crabbed towards the edge of the wharf. Safe on two sides; one she had her back against and the other taken up by the river; a proper quayside with mooring bollards and lifting engines, currently devoid of ships

Her eyes flickered back and forth across the yard, scanning for any sign of movement. The silver trail went halfway along the front of the wharf, then turned north and disappeared amongst the piles of goods. Exactly what Claire had hoped wouldn't happen.

She still couldn't see if there was a gate on the other side of the yard, but if she went into the jumbled stacks, the Morph could sneak out when she wasn't looking. She edged back up to the gate, and tried her luck the other side. There were more objects scattered along the north wall, but no silver trail, so she figured none of them could be the Morph. It seemed she also had a good view of the gate all the way along the north wall, so she could see if the Morph made a run for it. Three safe sides.

She started to slide herself along the north wall, trying to look in three directions at once and determined to stop as soon as she could see if there was another gate and go back to stand guard. About halfway along the wall she realised she was losing her view of the entrance, but still couldn't tell if the west wall was solid. She stopped, fuming at how fate was playing games with her, and tried to decide what the best option was.

Out of her line of sight, on the west side of the yard, something fell to the ground with a crash and there was the sound of motion. Claire moved without thinking, her instinct believing something was making a break for it through some door she hadn't seen yet, and she ran along the rest of the wall. As she cleared the edge of the stacks, she saw there was no gate, and that a pile of boxes had been knocked over. There was no trail of silver, and her heart sank as she realised she had been duped. Her shoulders sagged and she let the PPG dangle from one hand. While she had been chasing boxes, the Morph would have snuck out the gate and be far away by now. And she didn't have the breath left to chase after it. She put the PPG back in its holster and sighed before turning to start back towards the gate. She would try to keep after it, but she couldn't run any more.

The stack nearest to her exploded, pelting her with wood and apples. She felt the amulet flash warm against her chest as it deflected the missiles, but the sheer volume of material knocked her off her feet and pushed her back into the wall. A moment later, the next stack along rippled and flowed into the reptilian shape of an attacking Morph.

Claire was already moving, rolling to her right over and over until she heard the thump of the Morph's tongue striking somewhere behind her. Knowing she had one or two seconds before it could strike again, her next roll brought her to her feet and she dived into the stacks. She would use the Morph's own trick against it. A shower of splinters flew at her from the Morph's next punch, but the Kevlar deflected them. They seemed to get a lot closer, though. She jinked right, then left, then right again. The river was ahead of her. She was clawing the PPG out of its holster as she ran.

Behind her, she could hear the Morph barging through the piles of goods, throwing things aside in its hunger for her. It wanted her out of the way before it tried to escape. She hesitated for a second, then decided to gamble. She pushed at the stack nearest to her, collapsing it back into towards all the other produce, then broke for the east wall, turning so that she was running backwards. She crashed into the wall, winding herself, just as the Morph broke free from the mess in the middle of the yard. The PPG was ready in her hands, and tracked the target almost on its own. Her finger tapped the trigger three times, sending out a spread of glittering purple that crossed every line the Morph could take like a submarine firing torpedoes. Two hit the Morph at the same time and it sank to the ground as a pool of gel.

Claire drew in a deep breath, her jaw clenched hard and her heartbeat hammering in her ears as she tried to sort out everything that was whirling around in her head. She heard booted feet running towards her, and turned in time to see two Warriors run through the gate, PPGs raised and ready. They skidded to a halt when they saw Claire. One was, to Claire's surprise, Evie. Both grew wide grins on their faces. The one she didn't know, a bulky boy with a blond fuzz-cut, walked up to her with his hand out.

'First kill?' he asked.

'Second,' said Evie, loudly.

'First official kill,' said Claire as she shook the boy's hand.

'Whatever,' he said, chuckling. 'Welcome to the most exclusive club in the world.'

He waved, and walked away. Evie stepped forward once he had left. She looked uncertain, shifting her weight from one foot to the other, bottom lip caught between her teeth. 'That was pretty stupid.'

Claire nodded, but couldn't wipe the grin off her face. 'It's not like I meant to. I was only going to follow it.'

'Even got that wrong,' Evie was grinning too, now, and there was no malice in her words. She half raised her arms, looking shy and awkward, and Claire stepped forward into the hug. It was brief, but intense, and they turned and walked towards the gate. 'How are you feeling?'

'OK. Buzzing. Scared. Wonderful. Everything's a bit unreal.'

'Want me to say you're tired?'

'Why?'

Evie nudged her arm and pointed. Halfway up the street was a tall figure with wildly unruly hair and a look of near panic on his face. As soon as he saw them, Jack started forward, then stopped, then started walking again.

'Thanks, but I think I'm OK.'

Evie held out her hand, and Claire gave her a quizzical look. 'Your PPG,' said Evie. 'You can't jump home if you're carrying. I'll take it back to the Tower for you.' The quizzical look was replaced by a lopsided grin as she handed her weapon over, then Evie peeled away with a wave, disappearing into the crowd. Claire could hear her, telling everybody that everything was sorted and they could go back to work.

'I was really worried about you,' Jack said. 'I shouldn't have let you go.'

'Couldn't have stopped me.'

He looked down at her. 'Probably not. How are you feeling?'

Claire thought for a moment. 'Hungry. Hungry enough to eat a horse.'

'Around here, you might wish you were,' said Jack pulling a wry face. 'My treat?'

Claire looped her arm though his. 'Absolutely.'

FIFTEEN

Claire sat in the lounge with her parents, watching the evening news as she ate vegetarian spagbol from a plate on her lap. She wasn't really paying attention, until the words 'Evelyn Jones' seared in to her mind. Rich, red sauce sloshed towards the edge of the plate as she lunged for the remote. Her parents made questioning noises as she rolled the news item back to the beginning and she waved at them to be quiet as she pressed 'play'.

'Police are tonight looking for a college girl from Harland,' said the news anchor. A grainy photo that didn't really look like Evie, yet was still clearly her, flicked up behind the anonymous presenter. 'Evelyn Jones has not been seen for three days. Our reporter, Martin Ellis, spoke to her guardian.'

The whole picture cut away to a woman sitting in an office. She looked about the same age as Claire's mum but more harassed. Her hair was frizzed out and in need of a good cut and condition, and she needed to change the theme of her makeup. The worry in her eyes was genuine and sharp. Off camera a male voice started asking questions.

'I understand Evelyn has been living in care for some years. Does she have a history of running away?'

'No she-'

'Does she have a reputation for being in trouble with the police? Would that be why she has gone missing?'

'Evie has no record of involvement with the police.'

'Could this be gang related, Mrs Nixon. Or drugs?' the eagerness in the reporter's voice to associate Evie with something ugly made Claire feel sick with anger.

'Evie has never gone missing before,' said the woman Claire now assumed was the 'Smeggie Knicks' Evie had mentioned, and when the idiot reporter tried to interrupt her again, she drove right over him. 'She has a good record, and is working hard to finish a college course. An absence of this duration is totally out of character.'

The camera cut away to a follow-up shot of a male reporter with bouffant hair and a lary wide collar. 'There we have it. A vulnerable young woman, apparently lost under mysterious circumstance, desperately sought by police. Back to you in the studio.'

Claire pressed the button that let the PVR return to real-time, and sat back on the sofa, dinner forgotten. Evie had missed their last appointment, which had been on Wednesday. Claire had gone to the library again on the Thursday and Friday, but still no Evie. Today was Sunday, and perhaps now she had the 'why' – at least part of it.

'Why the big frown, squirt?' asked her father. 'You look like you saw a ghost.'

'Nothing. I mean, I thought I recognized the girl in the news, but I don't know the name. Made me feel a bit spooky, though.' She stood up and turned to her mother. 'Mind if I don't finish this. It's nice, but I don't feel hungry anymore.'

'Of course, not, sweetie,' said her mother, reaching out and rubbing Claire's hip. 'You can snack later if you change your mind.'

Claire dumped the plate in the kitchen and went up to her room. She didn't know what to do. She couldn't go to the police. What could she say? Nor did she have any way to contact Evie.

She had asked, twice, for a mobile number, but Evie had told her she didn't believe in mobiles. And she still couldn't jump in on her own.

It was two weeks since she had made her second kill. Evie had turned up every time she had said she would, but they had split up three or four hours in to each trip. Claire had been left to find her own amusement and her own way out. She had managed to find an excuse to spend most of the free time with Jack, but Evie had seemed increasingly distant, with her mind on something else.

Claire had even asked if Evie was getting bored with the training, or if she wasn't making enough progress. Evie had been really apologetic, saying that she was really busy at the moment and not to worry because they had another two months before Claire would get her final assessment. Except it wasn't, they were down to six weeks.

The missed appointments and this news item added up to something uncomfortable, but Claire couldn't shift the core-deep belief that the police were looking in the wrong place. What she could do about it was a different problem. There was nobody she could contact to jump her into Underland. Her closest option was to and try to get one of the geek squad at school to jump her in, but the shame would be unbearable and the chance of anybody actually helping her was zero.

She tried to jump to the spot in front of her locker over and over, and every day that passed left her more stressed and tearful. Her mother took to checking her temperature with her hand on Claire's forehead, and recommending she might like to try St John's Wort if she was feeling depressed about going back to school. Her father even offered a stock yet totally heartfelt 'you know you can talk to me about anything, don't you'. Claire wished she could tell them. Wished she could tell somebody. Wished she could tell Jack. At least he would believe her.

Why had she never swapped mobile numbers with him? She trawled for him on the internet and several social media sites, but the name was too common and there was never a picture that looked enough like him to take a chance on trying to make contact. When she finally had to admit defeat, the size of the sigh and the little wave of sadness that washed over her came as a surprise.

And that was what gave her the idea. What if jumping wasn't about concentration? What if it was about the connection you had with wherever you were trying to get? She put on her Warrior gear. Her jaw tightened up and the emo-deep funk that had collected around her blew away like smog. She was Warrior Stone, with two kills to her name before she was out of training and she could do this. She stood in the middle of the room, and tried to visualise the Observer post where Jack usually worked. She built it, focused on it, let it build around her and seep into her, and turned.

Nothing happened, but a moment later she realised that wasn't exactly true. She had felt something, like the expectation that always preceded a jump out. So was she on the right track, but maybe not quite in the right place? Jack had told her that the runners trained for months before they were trusted to jump on their own, building up the image of the jump room until it was burned into their minds, and that had made her feel a little better if no less frustrated. So what was sharper in her mind than Jack's office? A grin started to creep over her face as she let a new image build in her thoughts. She carefully edited out any time cues, and let it suffuse through her before she applied a twist and…

There were a few angry mutters from the small crowd around her, and a female Hrund was being helped from the floor where, presumably, the force of Claire's arrival had knocked her. Claire almost went to help before she realised that would make the situation worse. Instead, she bowed deeply. 'My profound apologies, Sa. This is an emergency.'

The Hrund gave her a displeased look, but then offered a curt nod of acknowledgement. Claire turned and hurried away into the underground station. She stood at the far end of the platform, shifting from foot to foot and doing a little two-step pace back and forth as she waited for a train. When it came in, she stood close to the edge and quickly touched the Warrior-only pad near the door before she stepped to the side and into the first carriage.

The ride, like the wait, seemed to take forever. When the doors did finally hiss open, Claire twisted to get through them as quickly as she could and was up the stairs and through the door before she heard the train pull away.

And then she was standing in the main corridor of the SFU offices, realising that she didn't have a clue what to do next. The locker room seemed an unlikely place to find anything useful, but she knew the way to that best. As usual, there was nobody else there, which was a quirk that Claire had never really understood. She walked up to Evie's locker. Next to the lock, somebody had stuck a yellow label. The label had no words on it, and there was a thin film of dust on top of the handle. It hadn't been opened in days. Claire looked closer and saw somebody had picked two of Evie's kill-markers off.

A hot flash of fury flickered over her. Something was very much not right.

It took her a while to find the stores. She had only been there once, but other than the posh office and the target range, it was the only other place she knew in the headquarters. She pushed through the correct door. All three gates were closed, and there was an oppressive silence hanging over the empty room. Claire was about to walk out when she noticed a tiny silver bell hanging from a piece of string tied to one of the railings. She walked up to it and gave it a gentle shake.

There was a distant muttering. She couldn't tell if it was one voice or several, but footsteps scuffled towards her from somewhere off to the left. Claire wished they would hurry up, but as she drew breath to call out a Grenlick walked out from behind a line of shelving. Only it wasn't who she had expected.

'What is this?' the Grenlick complained. 'Don't you people understand break times?'

'Sorry, there was nothing on the door.'

'So what do you want? Where is your requisition chit? I don't

117

have all day to waste while you dither.'

Claire tried to figure out a polite way to ask, then gave up. 'Look, I'm sorry if this offends anybody or anything and I know about the name thing and all that, but I need to speak to Krosset, and I need to speak to him now. Please. It's really urgent.'

The Grenlick glowered at her, and one side of its mouth lifted in either a sneer or a snarl, but it turned and wandered back into the shelving. Claire hoped it wasn't ignoring her and going back to its lunch. The shuffling paused for a moment, then started to get louder again, only this time the gait was heavier. After what felt like an eternity, Krosset stood at the middle gate and glared at her. 'I assume there is a very good reason for this?' He sounded offended.

'I know I busted about ten rules of proper behaviour, but I don't know everything yet, and I don't think I have time to find out. So can we please just leave it that I'm a bad person who hopes to do better? I really needed to speak to you. Evie has gone missing and I don't know who to talk to about it. I know it's not you, but I only know you so you were the only place I could start.' Claire realised she was babbling and forced herself to shut up whilst looking hopefully at the Grenlick.

Krosset lost his angry expression, which changed to something more understanding. 'It happens to all of you eventually,' he said. 'You should start by talking to Human Resources. Second floor, room 209. Next door to Personnel.'

'Thank you,' said Claire, already turning and walking away.

In the second floor office, only one of the three desks was occupied, and the Sathaari was not pleased at being distracted from the small meal in front of him.

'Please, it's really important,' Claire begged, and he dabbed daintily at the corners of his perfectly clean mouth with a napkin, before draping the napkin over his food as though he expected Claire to spray spittle over it.

'Very well,' he said with a theatrical sigh. 'What seems to be the problem?'

'Evie, I mean Warrior Jones, has been reported missing.'

'Yes.' It was drawled in a 'tell me something I didn't know' voice. The wind was sucked from Claire's sails and she did an impression of a stranded fish.

'You know?'

'I know that Warrior Jones has not reported for duty for a week. I know that she did not advise us in advance of any planned absence. I know that, given Jones' age, it is only a matter of time before she becomes unable to jump into Underland, and we assume this time has arrived.'

'No. You don't understand. Evie isn't in the Real. She's down here. She must be. They've reported her missing, to the police.'

'We have no evidence of that. Without any evidence, we must assume that Jones it still in the Real. Any issues or difficulties she may be experiencing there are beyond our jurisdiction. Now, if you wouldn't mind...?' He waved a hand across his napkin-covered plate and raised his eyebrows as if questioning Claire's continued presence in his office. Claire tried to speak, twice, but both times nothing came to her that had any chance of swaying the bureaucrat's mind, so she turned and left, closing the door gently behind her.

What could she do now? She knew so little about the non-physical side of the SFU, and apart from Evie and Krosset, she didn't know anybody else. Apart from Jack. She reached into her pocket for her communicator, pressed the blue gem to open a call, and spoke Jack's name. When he answered, she was still surprised by how clear the voices were on the little box.

'Hi. Where have you been?'

'Long story. I need to talk to you.'

'Sure, I'm off duty in about three hours.'

'No, sooner.'

'Okay,' his tone shifted to something placating, reacting to the tension in her voice. 'I can probably sneak out for fifteen minutes. Perhaps a half hour.'

Claire fumed. 'That'll have to do.'

'Where?'

Claire tried to think of somewhere close they both knew.

'The squash parlour on Harp Lane?'

'I know it. I'll be there as soon as I can.'

She closed the connection and set off.

At the cafe Claire ordered a pitcher of squash, then realised she had nothing to pay with and hoped Jack wouldn't mind. As a Warrior she would get paid, as a trainee she got nothing. She had finished her squash and was considering starting on his by the time he showed up. He took a seat next to her, ignored the squash, and got right to the point.

'What's such a panic?'

She told him about the missing person report, and what the Sathaari in Human resources had said. Jack sat back and looked thoughtful.

'I don't understand why you are so worried. If she is missing in the Real, then there's nothing you can do.'

'But she isn't. She's here. I know she is.'

'Know? How?'

Claire's lips made a tight, angry line. This was not going how she had expected. He was supposed to be her friend, to believe her. 'All right, I don't 'know' know, but she wouldn't get herself in any trouble in the Real. She's too smart for that and everything in her life revolved around Underland.'

'How long have you known her,' asked Jack, his tone like a grown-up about to make a point.

Claire could see where he was trying to go. 'Six months,' she said.

'More like two, if you take out the gaps. And you only know what she decided to tell you. You know everybody thinks she's slightly crazy, don't you?' Claire glared at him, and Jack had the grace to go red. It had been an unfair comment. 'I'm just saying you might not know her as well as you think.'

'And it sounds to me like you've made no effort at all. To know her, I mean.'

Jack shrugged. 'Maybe, but she never went out of her way to

120

be sociable. All she ever wanted to do was go around bursting Morphs.'

Claire scowled at him some more, then looked away. 'Whatever. I still think she is here, and she could need help.'

Jack sat back in his chair and picked up his squash. The Hrund chose that exact moment to come out and place the bill on the table. Claire blushed and wouldn't look at him, and eventually Jack chuckled and threw a couple of coins onto the bowl placed over the bill.

'This is really important to you.' Jack made it a statement,. Claire nodded and.Jack sighed. 'I honestly don't know what to suggest. Everything that goes anywhere goes through Aslnaff.'

Claire felt her shoulders droop, and pushed herself up from the chair. Jack rose too. 'I'm sorry about the squashes,' she said, waving a hand at the table. 'I'll pay you back someday.'

'Forget it.' Jack sounded like he was trying to make light, then he leaned sideways and gave her an awkward, quick hug.

Claire tensed up, surprised by the contact, and Jack froze, then jerked his arms away.

'Sorry, I…'

'Look, it…'

They spoke together, and both tailed off. Jack waved his hand to show he was waiting for her. 'It's not personal,' Claire said, quietly and with her eyes on the floor. 'I suppose I'm a bit edgy.'

Jack nodded and started to walk away from the parlour. 'Got to get back. Let me know how you get on.' He didn't turn, but threw a wave over his shoulder.

Claire watched after him, and was surprised to find she was furious. It took some thought to realise that she was more mad at herself than at Jack. That was not how it had been supposed to happen. They were supposed to be standing side by side watching trains from a bridge, or alone in a watch tower. And she certainly wasn't supposed to go spiky and brush him off. She gave him time to turn the corner at the end of the street before she set off in the same direction.

121

Sixteen

The next morning, she managed to jump in right in front of her locker, which came as a surprise. An envelope had been stuck to the locker. She peeled it off , but before she could open it she saw that underneath the envelope somebody had stuck two slightly second hand kill-stickers. A lump appeared in her throat as her hand reached out to gently run her fingers across them.

She took a deep, slightly trembling breath and opened the envelope, hoping it was a note from Evie. As soon as she saw the formal-looking cream paper, she knew it wasn't. It was addressed to 'Trainee Stone'.

'You are required to present yourself to the Administrator's office at your earliest convenience, or to arrange an appointment to do so, before you engage in any further training or operational activities for the SFU.'

It had the administrator's name at the bottom, with an illegible scrawl above it. Claire had read enough military fiction to know that 'earliest convenience' meant 'now', so she made her way up to the administrative offices and presented herself to the secretary. The Hrund kept her face absolutely neutral, but it was obvious that Claire was expected, and equally obvious that the Hrund knew why.

So did Claire. She had been asking questions, and rubbing people up the wrong way. She had gone from Post to Observation Post asking if anybody new anything about Evie's movements or activities. She had even been to the Central Police Station, right here in the same compound as the SFU building. Someone had told her she could speak directly to the Station Commander if a member of the SFU was being abused, but the chat with the Station Commander had escalated into a row, and she had – rudely she now admitted – jumped out in the middle of it.

Again, Aslnaff kept her waiting. She couldn't decide if it was some kind of punishment, if he was trying to show her how unimportant she was, or if people were genuinely busy.

But nobody went into the Administrator's office or came out before she was called, so she assumed the worst. She was so angry by the time she was told to go through that her jaw was clenched and she pulled the door open so hard she felt she might rip it off its hinges.

She walked up to the desk and stood in front of it. Aslnaff didn't look up, but shuffled papers back and forth on his desk and pretended to peruse one or two. Claire had seen this trick before, and she was beyond being polite.

'You asked to see me, Administrator,' she said, voice strong and clear and choosing her words very deliberately.

Aslnaff's head shot up. 'I *sent* for you, trainee. I sent for you because I will not tolerate any more of this foolishness about Warrior Jones. If Jones has experienced some difficulty in the Real, that is regrettable but beyond our jurisdiction and area of responsibility. If, as is far more likely given her age, Jones simply cannot enter Underland any more – well, it is unfortunate and perhaps you would pass on our appreciation for her efforts when you next see her. But Jones is not in Underland, in difficulty or otherwise, and I will not have you embarrassing me, or the rest of the SFU, with any further nonsense such as the regrettable incident with the Station Commander. I have no idea how you came by this arcane precedent, but whoever told you about it counselled you poorly.'

Claire's heart was hammering and her breathing deepened during Aslnaff's oration. Her lips had compressed into a hard thin line, and she could hear her breath whistling through her nose. She drew breath, ready to all but shout a defiant argument back at the administrator, but at the last second she bit her tongue. Was she being goaded? Was Aslnaff deliberately trying to push her into an outburst? Could he use that to throw her out? She let the breath out slowly, made a conscious effort to relax, and tried again.

'Sorry, Administrator. I'm only trying to act in the best interests of a fellow Warrior, and the SFU.'

Aslnaff blinked hard and looked surprised, and Claire smothered a smile. 'Yes, well,' the administrator blustered as he tried to rework his strategy. 'Laudable, I am sure, but-'

'Please, Ser.' The interruption earned Claire a look that made Aslnaff look like he was peering at an unsightly bug on the end of his nose. 'I understand that maybe nothing official can be done, but what about in my spare time? I would like to be allowed to look for Ev – Warrior Jones, or to see if I can find out anything about where she was last seen.'

Aslnaff sputtered for a moment. 'Absolutely not. The only reason any human has to be in the Under is performing their SFU duties. This is not some recreational resource for dilettante teenagers. Your actions could bring shame on the department. It is essential that you act within departmental policy at all times, and I fear that this part of your training has been neglected.'

He stopped and took a long, hissing breath through his nose as he pointedly rolled his shoulders. One hand briefly rose to smooth at what was left of his hair then rejoined its twin, interleaved on the desk. His voice was much calmer when he continued. 'I must say that I had grave doubts regarding Jones' somewhat grandiose plans for late-entry Warriors, and it would seem my concerns have been vindicated. However, you have made a contribution, and you obviously have some aptitude. Therefore, I am reassigning you to the grade of Junior Observer.

You will be assigned duty station and rotation accordingly, and it will be the responsibility of your assigned Senior Observer to ensure you are properly trained in the basics. Have to learn to walk before we can fly, eh?'

This last was delivered in a way that made Aslnaff come over like a creepy uncle, or a teacher trying to be 'dahn wit da yoof', and Claire would have been trying to stifle a laugh if it hadn't been such a transparent attempt to wind her up. In truth, she was tempted to simply throw in the towel, and had it not been Evie, she probably would have. For now, she felt she needed the SFU, and if this was the only way to keep that, then she had to bow down and take it. It still tasted very bitter.

'OK,' was the best she could manage without saying something she shouldn't. Again, the look of surprise on Aslnaff's face was some reward, even though this time it was tinged with suspicion.

'Very well. Inform stores of your change of status and they will arrange for your equipment transfer. You can turn in your Mk.22 and your goggles immediately.'

Claire hadn't thought of that, and she felt deflated. It was going to be much more dangerous moving around in Underland without her Warrior's equipment. Still, she nodded at Aslnaff, who was already looking down at the paperwork he had been pretending to study when she came in. He flicked his fingers dismissively at her. Biting the inside of her cheek, Claire turned and left the room as she tried to figure out exactly when it was she had decided to go look for Evie regardless of anything Aslnaff might have said.

SEVENTEEN

Krosset was manning the window of the stores when Claire entered the room. Someone she didn't know was being served so she hung back until they were done, exchanging a polite nod as they left. Krosset was giving her a very strange look as she walked up to the counter, carrying her PPG and her goggles.

'You heard?' she said.

Krosset nodded. 'More than you might think.' He took her gun and her goggles, and handed her a chit to say she had returned them. Claire smiled sadly and started to turn, but Krosset called her back. 'One moment, Warrior.'

Claire was surprised how good it made her feel to be called that. She turned back and looked questioningly at the Grenlick, but he seemed to be mulling something over and reluctant to speak. She waited. He usually had something worthwhile to say.

'Warrior Jones has a very odd number on the back of her Kevlar,' he said, seemingly at random. 'It's the opposite of yours, which is a total coincidence.'

'I suppose it is,' said Claire, keeping polite and trying to keep the bemusement off her face and out of her voice.

'People tend to be unimaginative when it comes to the security codes on their lockers. They tend to be lazy, and predictable.'

'I guess,' Claire agreed, eyes flicking guiltily away. Her own locker code was set to the same as the number on the back of her own amulet.

Krosset nodded sagely. 'Oh, they are. And very busy we are, too. You'll have to wait at least a week for us to reclaim the outstanding equipment from your locker. Administration will have to wait even longer for Warrior Jones' effects. She has to be out of contact for another three weeks before we can even raise the paperwork to put her things into storage.' He started shaking his head instead. 'Things can move so slowly sometimes.'

He pulled the shutter down and turned away, carrying off her weapon and her goggles, and waved over his shoulder. Claire looked at his receding back, trying not to let the slight grin playing around her lips gain too much purchase. She still had things to do inside the building. People would pay her too much attention if she didn't look chastened, if not positively depressed.

For the first time ever, the locker room was busy. She could see four observers in various aisles, and a conversation she had been able to hear from outside the door – shouted from row to row – fell silent as she entered. Claire sat on a bench as far away from everybody else as she could, head hanging, trying to look like she just wanted to be left alone. The observers gravitated towards each other, accreted into a knot, and started whispering to each other in scandalised tones as they migrated towards and through the door.

Claire waited until she heard the door clunk shut into its frame, then quickly checked the rest of the room. When she was sure she was alone, she stepped over to Evie's locker and used her own code, reversed. For a moment, Claire through Krosset had made a mistake as the door wouldn't open. After another experimental yank she realised it was sticking at the top. She pulled harder, with an extra tug downward, and the door popped open. Claire groaned. There was a huge mess of stuff on the shelf and on the floor but, to Claire's satisfaction, no duster coat and no PPG in the clip at the back. Evie was still in the Under.

There was too much to carry, but she had no time to sort through it all now. She ran over to her own locker and jerked it open. She had left a large shoulder bag inside a week ago and had forgotten to take it home. It was strong, made of black canvas, and would be able to carry most of Evie's stuff. She slammed her own door and ran back, cramming the bag with anything that didn't look like abandoned food, spare clothes, or litter. When she reached the bottom of the pile and prodded aside something that looked like it might have been an item of clothing, Claire gasped and stepped back.

Lying on the locker floor was a battered holster, and inside was a PPG.

She couldn't wear it. She was supposed to be nothing more than an observer now. On the other hand, she wasn't going to ignore such a stroke of good fortune. She stuffed it into the bag, packing other things around it to make the shape less obvious, then shut the door and walked out of the locker room.

Claire left the Tower by the private underground station, and took a train to Commercial Road. When she got off, she found Cotton Street easily enough, but all the little shops looked the same. She walked all the way along the street and peered at the front of each arch. Many she could ignore; they were open and either had display windows or goods out on the street. She could also eliminate anything too close to either end of the road as she had a clear recollection of walking some distance before Evie had started hammering on a door. That left four arches that seemed to offer the best chance of finding Tolks.

Someone was staring at her. Several someone's, and when she raised her head and looked around Claire realised that she had been drawing attention to herself. Walking up and down the street then standing and staring across the busy thoroughfare was not a particularly covert action, and she looked around guiltily. Would the SFU have spies out here? Would they be looking for her? She even shot a glance upwards, looking for any Observation towers. She ground her teeth and looked across the road; she had to get on with it.

Crossing the street, she went up to the first alcove and hammered on the door. As she did so, the Grenlick in the store to her left leaned out through his door and scowled at her as he hooked the bottom of his shutter and pulled it down. Claire made a face at the grating and hammered again. There was no answer.

She moved on to the next alcove. This one had no shutter, but there was no shop front either and the door, when she tried it, was locked. She knocked loudly, and was sure she saw a flicker of movement thought the translucent pane in the window. She knocked again, trying to make it sound as though she wasn't going to take no for an answer; a policeman's knock. She put her ear to the door. Scuffing footsteps drew closer, and she jerked away as the sound of rusty bolts scraped on the air. The door opened a few inches, held in place by a chain, and a suspicious face peered out of the gap.

That was when Claire realised she didn't know what to say. Grenlix were pathologically suspicious, and were so hung up about names that she couldn't think how she could ask for him without naming him. 'Grenlick,' she said and bowed her head, playing for time. The face cut her no slack.

'What?'

'I seek the Grenlick who works on this street,' Claire started, speaking slowly as she tried to weave the question. 'He works with others to repair things.'

'There are at least three,' said the face, and the door started to close. Claire managed to jamb most of her foot into the gap, and had a flashback to her first day on the job. In ballet pumps, her foot would have been crushed.

'The one I want works with others, very near here.'

'I don't know him,' said the face, and the door was slammed harder on to Claire's foot. 'Go away.'

Claire dropped her voice and tried to make it more menacing. 'I know his name, Grenlick, and I'm reasonably sure you do too.

Apart from messing with a Warrior, do you want me to tell him I had to stand out in the middle of the street shouting his name because you wouldn't tell me which shop was his?'

The face at the door looked a little less certain of itself, but no less hostile. It growled, spat at the floor next to Claire's foot, and a bony finger pointed to Claire's right. 'Four doors down, human.

Claire held eye contact as she withdrew her foot, and made no attempt to offer her thanks. The door slammed shut and Claire flipped her middle finger at it before moving down the street. When she reached Tolks' door, it did seem familiar now she knew it was the right one, and she hammered on it. 'Closed!' The voice was familiar, too, and Claire felt a flush of relief. She hammered again.

'It's Warrior Stone,' she said, loudly but not shouting.

'Still closed.'

'Don't make me start yelling your name out here,' she replied, letting her voice drop. It sounded like Tolks was on the other side of the door, and she didn't want to make the confrontation any more public than it had to be. That would just make things harder later. 'And don't make me start saying how much help Warrior Jones said you were.'

There was the sound of bolts being pulled back and the door creaked ajar. Claire eased it far enough open for her to slip through, then closed it behind her. She turned, raising her hand to slide one of the bolts back into place, but then she hesitated. Did she want to be locked in here? If things got nasty, could she still get out quickly enough? She dropped her hand to a smaller bolt and pushed it home. Enough to keep out casual visitors, but she hoped she would be able to pull the door open despite it if she had to. She turned and made her way across the gloomy outer shop, towards the door to the workspace at the back.

Tolks stood in the middle of the workshop, arms crossed in front of him and feet firmly planted at shoulder width. He did not look happy, and the three youngsters sitting at the bench were very careful to make it very obvious they were not paying any attention at all.

'That was not appropriate,' said Tolks, glowering. 'One does not threaten one with whom names had been exchanged.'

Claire was still thinking on the run, but now she was getting tired. 'Then you could try answering a knock on the door with something other than 'Closed'. Give me a break, will you? I've only been here for a few weeks. I need to talk to you and I have nobody to ask on the finer points of Grenlick etiquette.'

'Perhaps I was hasty-'

'Yes, you were.'

'Hasty in assuming you were a person worthy of sharing names. It seems Warrior Jones still has some way to go with your training.'

'And I wouldn't need to do this if I could ask her. Ev... Warrior Jones has gone missing.'

'An accident Above? Such a shame.' Tolks was already turning away, and Claire couldn't decide if he somehow already knew, or had already been told that was what he was supposed to say. She felt very unsure of herself. She had no friends down here, apart from Jack and Evie, and maybe Krosset. The enormity of what she was trying to do began to loom over her, threatening to topple and crush her. But Evie trusted Tolks, and if Evie trusted him, she would have to have a good reason. She decided to take the chance. After all, she had no other lead to follow.

'Evie isn't in the Real. Wherever she is, she's down here.'

Tolks stopped and turned back. 'What makes you say that?'

'Many things. Mostly that loads of her stuff wasn't in her locker.'

'Not convincing.'

'Her PPG was missing, and her holster, plus her goggles and coat and all the other equipment she took out with her when she was here. Evie would never take anything like that Above. She would never do anything she could get kicked out for.'

Tolks unfolded one arm and stroked his chin with a hand. 'Interesting, but still not convincing. There is much that could

132

explain her absence, or the absence of her belongings. Someone could have stolen them.'

'Really? Can you imagine what Jones would do to anyone she caught stealing from her?'

A flicker of a smile ghosted around Tolks lips. 'Also true.' Again, he turned away, but he stepped only so far as to climb onto a stool. The workbench was set apart from the long one used by the others. There was less clutter here, and only a small number of devices. Claire guessed it was Tolks own bench. He flicked a cloth out to cover what he had been working on, and waved Claire towards another stool.

'Can you tell me anything?' Claire pleaded. 'Evie said she trusted you. Did she tell you anything that might explain where she is?'

Tolks was already shaking his head before Claire had finished talking. 'I'm pleased that Warrior Jones trusted me, and it is precisely because she trusted me that I could tell you nothing even if I knew anything that would be of help to you. What worth would my trust be then?'

'But not even if she's in trouble?'

'I am sure you have the best intentions, but the path to chaos is paved with such. Without being sure that Jones would want, or need, me to share her secrets with you, I cannot help.'

Eighteen

Claire felt her bottom lip pout out like a baby's, and she hurried to cover the sulk with a frown. 'So what am I supposed to do? The SFU say she's forgotten how to jump in, and the police say there isn't any evidence to prove she is still in Underland, so they don't want to know either. Am I supposed to forget about it and go home? Leave her?'

Tolks eyebrows had clicked out sideways. 'So, it would seem, many want you to think.'

'Pardon?'

'Does it not strike you as odd that nobody is even prepared to consider the possibility that Warrior Jones might be in Underland?' Tolks shook his head. 'I fear that this pot is one too deep for me to want to stir, and I wonder if you are wise to do so.' He rubbed at his nose. 'I can offer you this. If Jones has left such titbits as will lead you on to more, then that is her concern and I betray no confidences. Jones has a room, here in Underland. It is on an outside wall of Hive Straknat, which you will find at the corner of Felton St and Harvey St. The information is reasonably well known, but not the detail. Enter through the door at that corner. Go no further than that room. Ask for 'the Grenlick Hivemaster', but accept a subordinate.

That is all I can offer you.'

Claire looked steadily at Tolks, then nodded. It was less than she had hoped to get out of him. She had hoped that Evie's friendship would count for more, and that the Grenlick would summon a posse of street-wise helpers and start scouring the city for clues. What she had been offered was better than nothing, though. She slid off the stool and made her way to the front of the shop, the only other sound the muffled shuffle of Tolks' feet behind her. At the door, she turned.

'What is the right way to ask for you?' said Claire.

Tolks wiry eyebrows rose fractionally and the corner of his mouth quirked upwards for a second. 'Without a Warrior's uniform often works better.'

Claire nodded, and bowed formally. Tolks returned the bow with equal gravity. 'Good luck, Warrior Stone.' Claire opened the door, walked outside, and heard it close gently behind her.

And now she was on the street, wondering where the hell Felton St and Harvey St were. She reached into her pocket and pulled out her communicator. Jack would know. She held the communicator in her hand, but didn't speak to it. Jack would want to know why, and if she didn't tell him, he would probably be sitting at the corner waiting for her. She wanted to tell herself that she didn't want to get him into any trouble. She also wanted to believe that he wouldn't tell anybody where she was, or push her to find out what she was doing. Her thumb lifted away and she put the box back in her pocket.

She walked back to the underground station, keeping an eye out for a policeman. Evie had told her once that they knew how to get just to about everywhere. When she found one, he was an Angel, walking along the opposite side of the street, and heading towards her. She crossed over, dodging past a cart being pulled by a steam 'donkey' and an omnibus, and stood out of the way on the other pavement. As the officer stepped into speaking distance, Claire took a half-step forward and said 'Excuse me,' but the Angel walked straight past without even looking at her. Claire reached out, grabbing at his arm and calling 'Hey.'

A metallic, electric jolt made her hand and arm jerk like a static shock. The Angel twisted away with a snarl in his own language that was unmistakably cursing, and as he turned back to her his hand was already drawing his nightstick from a loop on his belt. Claire, horrified by what was happening, stepped back and raised her open hands to show she was carrying no weapon.

'Idiot! Are you so stupid you forget the effect of your touch or so arrogant you do not care who you injure?'

Claire knew there was no good answer to that question.

'I'm really sorry. I forgot.'

'Forgot? A warrior?'

If she said she was only a trainee, then she would be drawing attention to herself, and that would not be a good idea. 'You walked straight past me. You want to talk to me about manners?' She made a point of looking at the constable's shoulders, as if trying to see his official number. She was too short, and the Angel seemed to realise this and stood up straight. 'What did you want?'

'Directions. I need to get to Felton St.'

'I know no such place,' said the Angel, and he started to turn away. Claire stood her ground and cleared her throat, and he stopped. 'What? What would you have me say?'

'You're a constable. You have no idea?'

He pulled an angry face. 'And I care less. Take the underground west, perhaps to Broad Street. Ask again there.'

This time he walked off without another glance. Claire let him go. It wasn't a bad idea, but this individual had not been what she had expected. All the other police she had met with had at least been professional, if not courteous. But then, this was the first Angel constable she had encountered, and she wondered if they were all so rude. She shrugged and walked down to the trains.

On the advice of a more public spirited policeman at Broad Street, Claire left the underground at a station called Arlington Square, and found Felton St on the south side of Branch Bridge.

The outward appearance of Hive Straknat was almost a copy of where Tolks lived, with even more shops around the edges. Here, though, there were more people milling around, and the shops were patronised not just by other Grenlix, but by Hrund and Sathaari. She worked her way along the side of the building, looking up at the small, forbidding windows ranked along the wall above her and wondering if Evie's 'room' was behind one of them. She hoped so. There was something uncomfortable about the idea of going too deep inside the hive or, worse, under it.

At the end of Felton St, on the corner of the building, was a doorway. It was set back into the angle of the corner: strong double doors with heavy hinges and iron banding riveted across them. One side was open and there was a steady stream of Grenlix moving to and fro. To her surprise, while she was watching, a Hrund also walked in, and an Angel stepped out, looking nervously back and forth before disappearing into the crowd. Apparently, it wasn't only the shops that were more cosmopolitan.

When there was a gap in the traffic, Claire stepped through the door. Inside there was another pair of doors, like an airlock. These were also open and led to a hallway. It stretched the height of the building, with balconies around each floor above. Hrund stood guard at each arched exit and at the stairwells, one on either side of the hall. The floor was tiled in a heavy grey stone that looked rough and gritty and the walls were panelled with dark wood. Although there were windows along two walls of each balcony, the hall was gloomy, and the magic-fed lights that dotted the walls only seemed to make the shadows deeper.

A window set into one of the wooden walls looked like it might be an enquiry desk. There was a narrow shelf in front of it, a light directly above it, and a door set off to the side that was almost hidden in the design of the panelling. She marched across to the window, trying to look official. A beige shutter had been pulled down behind the window, but there was an old fashioned bell with a plunger on top. Claire grinned; she had always wanted to have a go on one of these. She slapped it smartly, twice, and waited. The shutter rolled up with a snap and a female Grenlick looked through the window. 'Yes?'

Claire was already standing up as tall as she could and had her serious face on. 'I would speak with the Grenlick Hivemaster.'

'Do you have an appointment?'

'This is SFU business. Do I really need one?'

The Grenlick behind the counter looked at her for what felt like an age and Claire hoped her bluff wasn't going to get called. She had nothing to back her claim up with, and if it was checked, she would just be dropping herself in deeper trouble.

'Wait here,' the female snapped and the shutter was pulled down as energetically as it had been allowed to fly up. Claire stood in front of the window and waited. Then she stood beside the window and waited, her back to the wall and glaring back at anybody curious enough to stare at her as they passed. Eventually, the unobtrusive door opened and a male Grenlick stood in the opening. Claire walked over to him.

'I am the Assistant Duty Hivemaster?' He seemed tense, as though he was expecting to be rejected or dismissed, but Claire nodded and he stepped aside to let her in to what turned out to be a small, bare room with a table and four chairs. The wall to her left was another door, presumably opening into the office behind the window. 'What is your business?' he asked once they were seated.

She had been thinking about this while she had been waiting. 'I am here on behalf of Warrior Jones. She requires something from the room your Hivemaster has been kind enough to offer her.'

'This is not our concern.'

Claire nodded. 'Of course, but it would be rude of me to simply walk in and wander around without asking your permission and, to be honest, I would appreciate a guide to show me where the room is. The directions Warrior Jones gave me were... unclear,' and she smiled to let the Assistant Duty

139

Nobody know she was letting him in on a little secret. His expression didn't change, so she wasn't sure it had worked, but after a moment he nodded.

'Your consideration is appreciated. If you wait here for a moment I will guide you myself.' He stepped through the door into the office, there was a muted conversation, and he reappeared – this time wearing an overcoat. He opened the outer door and gestured to Claire. 'Would you follow me, please?'

Claire followed him out of the room, past the guards at the bottom of one of the staircases, and up two levels. From there, they went through a door that Claire thought pointed back up Felton St. She wasn't sure what she was expecting, but she felt nervous as the door swung open in front of her.

It took her eyes a few minutes to adjust. The light level behind the door was even lower. The wall sconces were yards apart and bore only tiny glowing balls. The walls looked as though they were made of brick, and curved overhead like a tunnel. The air was humid, and slightly tropical. Doors opened off one side of the wall, each next to or opposite one of the infrequent lights. On the other side of the corridor Claire saw more corridors stretching off, again with doors. There were muted sounds of speech, and brighter sounds that might have been children playing, but nobody came out of any door she could see. The corridors vanished into the distant shadow, and Claire guessed they went the entire length of the building.

A few steps later they stopped outside a door close to the corner of the building. There was an uncomfortable pause and neither of them moved for a moment. Eventually, Claire said. 'The door, please?' She had no idea if it would be locked or not, and she certainly didn't have any kind of a key. Breaking it down was an option if the lock wasn't too strong, but she had been hoping that wouldn't be needed. She was already drawing too much attention to herself, and making this undermanager let her in would be a much better idea if she could pull it off.

'But...?' the Grenlick said, looking slightly panicked. Claire kept still, trying to stare him down, and make him think she had no intention of going anywhere until he had opened the door for her. Eventually, he lowered his eyes. The set of his jaw made it clear he didn't like being treated this way, but he reached into a pocket and took out a short rod. It was matt black, and seemed to absorb what little light there was. Claire didn't like it, and felt a shudder run along her spine.

The Grenlick slid the rod gently into a matching hole in the door and there was a positive click from somewhere near the handle. He turned the knob and pushed the door open. Claire took two steps inside then turned, holding onto the door and blocking the way for the undermanager. 'Thank you. I can find my own way back from here.'

'But —?'

'Sorry, this bit is confidential. Warrior-only classified.' Claire felt her powers of improvisation starting to run out of ideas, and she wanted to bustle the Grenlick away as fast as she could. 'Or you can wait outside, if you must?' she added.

The Assistant Duty Hivemaster shook his head. 'That won't be necessary. If that's all?'

Claire smiled. 'You've been most helpful. I shall be sure to tell Warrior Jones.'

The Grenlick bobbed a bow and scurried away. Claire shut the door. There was a bolt inside, and she pushed it across. The room was almost in darkness. A little weak daylight managed to struggle around the edges of the heavy drape over the window. She pulled the curtain aside and went around turning on all the lamps she could find but it didn't make much difference. She picked her torch out of her pocket and started to search.

There wasn't much to look through. There was a single bed, with a table beside it, and a wardrobe with a drawer at the bottom. Next to the wardrobe was a small table with a single chair. The floorboards were bare wood and the walls were like those outside. With the slightly better light, she could see that the brickwork was fake, like textured wallpaper.

Claire checked the bed first, plumping the pillow and lifting the mattress to check that nothing was hidden within or beneath.

141

Next, she pulled open the drawer, and found a change of clothes, a towel and a wash bag. The wardrobe itself was equally uninteresting and contained even less; a few lonely hangers and a pair of boots. There was a built in shelf, just above Claire's eye-line, but when she stood on tiptoe and swept her hand across it, all she got was a layer of grey dust on her sleeve. She brushed at it, irritated, as she looked around the room. Surely there had to be more to see than this?

She opened the drawer again and had another look, gingerly rummaging through and giving each garment a closer inspection. It wasn't something she was comfortable with, messing with somebody else's underwear, but she picked up every item and shook it before putting it back on the other side of the drawer. Last, hidden in the corner, was a pair of socks twisted into a ball. Claire was about to drop them on the other pile when something felt wrong in her hand. She squeezed the socks again, and something inside crinkled. Claire took the socks over to the bed and unrolled them. Nothing fell out, but something still made a noise. She turned each sock inside out, and from one fell a slip of paper.

There was something written on the paper, and Claire turned it over and smoothed it out. She could make out the letters, but they made no sense. Disappointed, she folded the paper and tucked it away in a pocket. So far, it looked like she had already reached a dead end. She turned around and sat on the bed so hard she bounced, lips pursed in frustration and shoulders slumped. It was so annoying. She saw more dust on her sleeve and angrily brushed it away as she glared at the wardrobe. The strokes got slower then stopped. There was something nagging her about the top of the cupboard.

NINETEEN

When Claire was a little girl, she had always felt an irresistible urge to know what she was getting for Christmas. She would search high and low, especially in places she wasn't supposed to go. Every cupboard and closet, every drawer and wardrobe, was investigated in case secrets had been concealed within. Then, one year, it had stopped. All the presents had disappeared and she distinctly remembered that everybody had been going around looking smug as she got more and more frustrated. She hadn't been able to find a single thing, and every present that year, and the next, had been an absolute surprise.

And all this was coming back to her because the wardrobe in Evie's room looked very similar to the one that had been tucked away in the spare room of her grandparents' house. The wardrobe was where she had eventually found her presents. Crossing the room, Claire prodded at the chair to check it would take her weight, placed it next to the wardrobe, stepped onto it, and reached up.

There was a deep decorative edge running all the way around the top, leaving a space three inches deep that was hidden from the ground. Claire swept her arm back and forth, but all she collected was more dust. She moved the chair to the other side and tried again. Her fingers brushed something and she stretched as far as she could to get a better grip. At first it was still too far away to lift, but she managed to get enough contact to drag it closer. This time her fingers felt a cube, about three inches across, and she stretched her fingers over it to pick it up. Something inside moved.

The chair wobbled, and Claire decided to jump rather than step down to the floor. She took the box over to the window where the light was best. It was made of a pale wood with an open, smooth grain that looked to be about the colour of unstained beech. She tilted the box gingerly from side to side, trying to make the contents slide about. Whatever it was, there was only one. She turned the box over and over, but there was nothing identifiable as a lid, and she began to wonder if it was a puzzle. She went back to the bed, sat down, and started trying to figure the way in.

It wasn't easy. She managed to make one face move a fraction of an inch, but it didn't seem to release any of the other sides. The light had almost completely faded from the room before Claire realised she had overstayed her welcome. She checked her watch and gasped. Thirteen hours; two longer than she had ever stayed before. She tried to stay calm. She didn't know what her snap-back limit was yet. She would probably be fine, but this trip had gone over ten hours and she had to be getting close.

She was carrying too much equipment to just jump out, but she didn't want to spend the time taking it back to SFU headquarters. If she did, there was a good chance they would confiscate it. She looked at the cupboard and narrowed her eyes. She had an idea, but it relied on her being able to get in and out of this room without causing a fuss every time. That meant she needed to be able to jump directly here, and she didn't feel totally confident. Time and options were running out on her. She stripped out of her Warrior clothes and hung them in Evie's wardrobe. At least that would let Evie know she was being looked for if she was in hiding or something. She was about to put the PPG and the holster on the shelf, but she thought better of it. Climbing on the chair she put the weapon on the top of the wardrobe and pushed it back almost as far as she could reach, then put the chair back by the table. She started to jump out, remembered to grab the box at the last instant, and snapped back into her bedroom.

An hour later Claire had broken the secret of the box. The last movement was a little vigorous and whatever had been inside flew halfway across the room then slid across the laminate floor and disappeared under the pedestal of her computer desk. Claire swore under her breath and jumped after it. The unit was on castors but there was so much junk stacked between it and the underside of the desk that Claire thought twice before moving it. There was a good chance everything would slide to the floor and she would have one or other of her parents calling up the stairs to see if she was all right.

Taking a ruler from the top drawer, Claire swept it back and forth under the pedestal. The first sweep recovered a mint humbug – still wrapped - and half a rich tea biscuit. The second made a ball that belonged to the family cat roll forth. The third, with the ruler held by the very tips of her fingers, flicked out a locker key on a wrist strap. Claire was about to try a fourth time, but she stopped and scowled at the key. It wasn't hers.

The biscuit went in the bin. Marmaduke's ball was left where it was; he was perfectly capable of hiding it again whenever he wanted to. The key and the humbug were taken back to the bed. When she unwrapped it, the sweet was sticky but it was still within the boundaries of edible, so she sucked on it while she looked at the key.

The thick plastic strap was scratched and battered and a hideous yellow. Claire turned it over in her hands, and even put it around her wrist. There were some marks that might have been writing, but they were too faint to read. She sighed, dropped the strap onto her bedside table and fell back onto the bed. It was only eleven in the morning, but she had been up for hours – very busy, stressful hours – and she felt drained. With her legs still dangling over the side of the mattress, she closed her eyes. Just for a minute.

The smell of warm food hung heavily in the air when she woke, and the light coming in through her windows confused her for a moment, telling her indistinguishably it was first thing in the morning and early evening. Looking at the clock on the bedside table didn't help. It told her 7:22. Her stomach cramped, and hunger made the time a moot point. She set off in search of the food.

It was still Saturday, and the food was evening dinner, which on this occasion was a vegetable pasta bake with garlic ciabatta bread and ice cream for dessert. They ate off lap-trays, watching the television. Claire devoured the meal and fielded parental small talk asking if she was feeling OK and was there anything going on at school she wanted to talk about.

'After all,' said her mother. 'I know teenagers are supposed to enjoy their sleep, but napping all through the day isn't like you.'

'Honestly, Mum. I'm fine. I've been reading a really good book and I guess I stayed up a bit too late a bit too often.'

Her mother looked unconvinced but didn't press. All Claire wanted to think about was the key and the strap it was on. It had to be important, no matter how random it seemed. Evie wasn't the type to keep pretty boxes, even if they were clever and tricksey. She was even less likely to keep something like the key unless it was important. The more she thought about it, the more she realised she needed to find the locker the key belonged to.

The 'how' was going to be the trick. Evie had never talked about where she lived, not after the awkward conversation over milkshakes. The news item had mentioned Harland, in Hertfordshire, but there had to be a dozen sports centres Evie could have gone to nearby. Or maybe, she thought, Evie had gone even farther afield, trying to shake off anybody who was trying to follow. She pushed the thought aside before it could overwhelm her, and focused on what she could do. As soon as

146

she could comfortably excuse herself after dinner, she hurried back to her room and hit the 'net.

The first thing she did was go back over all the news articles she could find on Evie's disappearance. Nobody was reporting anything new, and all the police were saying was that they 'were expecting a significant development'. Claire just wanted any photos or videos of reporters. It seemed the fashion these days was for 'on the scene' reporting and she hoped she might see a street sign. The newer stuff was all useless. It had been shot outside a police station somewhere, so Claire went further back. She dug for two hours, and still came up with nothing. Not a single shot from any news service showed a street with a name. She was still no closer to finding out where Evie lived.

Giving up didn't feel like an option, so Claire turned the problem around and did a search on sports facilities within five miles of Harland. There were twenty-two, ranging from big sports centres to school swimming pools, private and public. Far too many to check each of them in person. Not without taking weeks.

Claire stood up from her desk, arched backwards to de-kink her spine and dropped onto her bed. She rubbed her face with her hands and scrubbed at her scalp with her fingers, frustrated and feeling tired again. She found herself looking at the wrist strap on her bedside table. She reached for it, turning it over in her hands and rubbing her finger softly over faint outlines. They were so nearly legible. She held it up to the light, twisting it this way and that, trying to make the shadows and highlights resolve into something understandable. She narrowed her eyes for a moment, grinned, and got up from the bed. Time to use some new technology in an old-fashioned way.

The strap got placed under the lid of the all-in-one printer next to her desk. There was a trick you could do with a soft pencil to bring up hidden words on paper. Perhaps she could do the same sort of thing digitally. She hit the 'scan' button. The printer whirred into life, the app opened on her pc, and in a couple of minutes a high-res scan of the outside face of the wrist strap appeared on the screen. Claire started playing, adding filters, changing colour channels, light balances, contrast and saturation levels. She fiddled with the images for a half hour before she admitted there was nothing there – at least, nothing she would be able to see this way. She turned back to the printer and opened the lid. The strap fell to the floor, and as she picked it up she realised she had only scanned the outside. Groaning softly, she put the strap in the other way up and started again. Ten minutes later she was looking at the screen with a mixture of disbelief and triumph, struggling not to drum her feet on the floor in celebration.

Clearly picked out from the inside of the bracelet she could see 'H.B.C.S&L'.

It took a single internet search to discover this stood for 'Harland Borough Council, Sports & Leisure Department'. The key came from a public facility, not a private one, and that narrowed the search down to five possible locations. Assuming, of course, that the first 'H' did mean Harland. There had been matches for Haringey, Huddersfield, and a dozen more places beginning with H, but at least she had a place to start. She printed off a map, and went to bed trying to figure a way to get herself to Harland in the morning without her parents getting suspicious.

Over breakfast she announced that she felt stiff and lazy and she was going for a ride on her bike.

'That sounds like a nice idea,' her mother said. 'Shall we all go? Where were you thinking of?'

Claire panicked. She hadn't expected that. Her mother usually worked over the weekend, or at least sat in the shop in case somebody drove in. They rarely did anything as a family on Saturday or Sunday. She put on a bright face. 'That would be nice. I was thinking of cycling up the canal path to Harland.'

Her mother flinched, and she was sure she heard her father chuckle quietly from the other end of the table. Mother's idea of a bike ride was a half hour, or an hour at most, and ended at a pub for lunch. The trip to Harland was at least twice that one way. 'Are you sure? You haven't been out much recently. You don't want to overdo it.'

Claire smothered a smile. 'I'll be fine. Mum. I want to work some kinks out. Are you sure you don't want to come?'

Her mother's head shook emphatically. 'I'd only slow you down. Have fun. Just remember you have to come back as far as you go.'

'I will,' Claire promised and stuffed the last of her peanut buttered toast into her mouth before swilling down the remains of her orange juice. The ensuing texture and taste in her mouth was – interesting.

She rode only as far as the train station. She had never had any intention of cycling all the way to Harland, or back. She had cash enough for a return ticket, and she didn't have time to waste. From Harland station she headed off towards the closest sports facility on her map, three miles away in the town centre.

She found a locker to fit the key at the third facility. It wasn't in the ladies changing room, but was outside the gym. It was smaller than the ones in the changing rooms, and the door flew open when she turned the key. The bag inside - black faux-leather with a mildly popular brand logo on the side - was too big for the locker and had exploded outwards almost half its length. Claire dragged the bag out, remembered to take the 50p from the slot, and closed the door.

There were a couple of benches just outside the centre and Claire eyed them indecisively. Part of her wanted to sit down and open the bag. There could be something obvious, right on the top. Maybe even something urgent so she had to jump in straight away. She even took two steps towards the benches before she realised the people inside the sports centre could be watching her. Jaw set in frustration, she slung the bag over her shoulder and set off to the train station.

Twenty

Claire was sitting on the bench outside the toilets. She had finished her lunch and was trying to read from her e-book. Her mind kept drifting back to Evie's bag, still unopened in her closet. Her parents had come home while she was still in the shower, and the rest of the day had been commandeered by an impromptu visit to friends. By the time they had returned, it was too late to start poking about in the bag. It had taken Claire ages to get to sleep, so the day was doubly cursed with fatigue and distraction.

Claire looked up. Melanie Styke was walking towards her, complete with a couple of the older girls in her group and a boy Claire recognised as an observer. She couldn't remember his name, but she was sure he didn't go to her school. There was something in the way Styke was holding herself that made Claire sit up and put her book away.

When Styke stopped she was well inside the boundary of Claire's personal space. Claire had left it too late to stand up so all four of them loomed over her and she couldn't shake the sense of intimidation that mixed with the anger growing inside her.

'What is this Styke? Piss off or-'

'This is official, Stone, so I suggest you shut your mouth and listen for a change.'

Claire looked up at the boy and he gave her a small nod. She tried to relax and settled back. Styke took a many times folded sheet of paper out of a pocket and shook it until it unfurled. She started to read from it.

'By order of Aslnaff, Administrator of the Special Facilities Unit, Claire Stone is hereby given notice that she has been suspended from the SFU pending investigation related to actions unbecoming a member of the Unit and in contradiction to both Unit written procedures and specific instructions given to her by lawful officers of the Unit. Ms Stone is hereby required to attend a hearing of the council of the SFU in two weeks, at SFU headquarters. If Ms Stone enters Underland anywhere other than the Administrative offices, she does so without the protection of the SFU or any other authority.

'Ms Stone is required to surrender any and all devices in her possession to the bearer of this notification.'

Styke re-folded the paper and looked up. 'So I'll have that Kevlar off you for a start,' she said, vicious grin wide on her face.

'Like hell you will,' said Claire as she tried to get to her feet, but the two older girls took a step forward and one put a hand on her shoulder, pushing her back onto the seat.

'Don't,' the boy said and everybody froze, not sure who he was talking to.

'I don't have it with me,' said Claire. 'You know the regulations on taking artifcact out of Underland.'

'Crap. You're wearing it. We're all wearing them.'

'You can't take it from me. Try and I'll scream loud enough to get a teacher over here and the whole lot of you will be done for bullying.' She scowled specifically at Styke. 'And they'll rip that prefect's badge off you.'

Styke laughed. 'Think so. Who do you think they'll believe? A prefect, or a weirdo like you?'

The boy turned to Styke. 'If you try to force her to hand it

152

over, I'll back her. And I don't care if you grass me up to Aslnaff, Shite. I'm here because its official, but I don't have to like it. Or you.' He turned back to Claire. 'Look, I know she's evil spawn, and getting off on this, but it is official. If you don't hand it over, they'll booby trap it.'

'How?'

'Not sure. Never happened before as far as I know. Supposed to be they act like Tasers if you jump in anywhere except headquarters. You get frozen until someone comes and releases you.'

'You must have heard about Warr-'

'Not my problem.' The boy interrupted, and his face went from helpful to blank in an instant. 'Look, in a month or so you won't remember anything about any of this, so what does it matter?'

Claire looked up at Styke, holding her gaze as long as she could, desperately trying to think of anything she could do other than give in, but she came up blank. Reluctantly, she raised her hands and feet for the clasp at the back of her neck.

Styke's expression shifted toward triumphant as Claire lifted the amulet out from under her shirt, and the prefect held her hand out, eyes shining greedily. Claire started to move her hand forward then snatched it back, now wearing a grin of her own.

'Where's my receipt.'

'What,' Styke snapped, annoyed.

'If I was handing this into stores, I'd get a receipt. I want one from you.'

'Oh, stop screwing around and give it to me.'

'She has a point,' said Claire's inconsistent advocate, and there was a general rummaging about as someone found paper and someone else donated a pen. By the time a suitable document has been scrawled out, Claire had found enough room to get to her feet. She had no intention of running. If what they were saying about the amulet was true there was no point keeping it anyway, but she was not going to let Styke screw her over like this while she was sitting down like a victim.

153

'Now give me the Kevlar.' Styke was almost shouting as she held out the tatty piece of paper. Claire snatched it out of her hand and made a show of reading it. 'Your handwriting looks like a six year old's,' she said, 'but it's close enough. Here.' And she flicked the amulet on to the floor at Styke's feet.

'Clever,' said Styke, but she still bent over to pick it up. Claire was already walking away, but she walked just close enough so that with a swing of her hips she sent Styke sprawling onto the gravel. There was a chuckle mixed with Styke's outraged shriek. 'I'll get you for that, Stone.'

'Any time, *Runner*,' said Claire, waving airily over her shoulder, and she was sure she heard the chuckle again. She took the first entrance she found back into the school, then headed for the nearest toilet. By the time she got there her whole body was shaking and spasms of pain dug into her kidneys as her back muscles clenched. She stood in front of a sink, looking at herself in the mirror. Her face was white apart from two spots of pink over her cheek bones. Splashing cold water on her face didn't help, and she felt dizzy. A moment later her lunch was in the sink and she was washing out her mouth at the water fountain.

Sitting down in one of the cubicles, she jammed the door shut with her foot and dropped her head into her hands. It had been so humiliating, and what was she going to do about Evie? The first sob came despite everything she tried to stop it, and after the first broke through, she had no chance of stopping the others. She cried, silently, sitting on the toilet until the bell rang for lessons. More cold water on her face from the sink did little to hide the red from around her eyes. She grimaced at herself in the mirror before she set off for her next class.

TWENTY ONE

It was Wednesday before Claire turned her attention back to the bag, and that was only with the intention of trying to find a way to dispose of it and its contents. She had been avoiding even thinking about it since Monday, and she had been doing her best to avoid any news broadcasts on the TV or the radio; anything that would remind her that Evie was still missing and that there was nothing she could do about it.

She felt terrible, like something had its hands around her heart and her lungs, and was squeezing so hard every breath and every heartbeat felt like a conscious effort. Both nights had been plagued with dreams of suffocating or drowning and she had woken gasping for breath. Trying to get back to sleep had been impossible. Every time she had been about to drop off, it felt like her heart missed a beat, or an exhalation took too long to become an inward breath. By Wednesday night, she decided she had to do something. She had almost fallen asleep in class twice, and her bed was calling to her now, even though she was terrified of it.

So after dinner she went up to her room, claiming homework to be done, and pulled the bag out of its hiding place. Her first thought had been to simply sneak out to the garden and dump the thing into the waste ground at the back of their property. It had the advantage of being simple, but Claire realised she had no idea what was in the bag. There could be artefacts from the Underland or, worse, something that was identifiably Evie's. If the police found it they would be crawling all over the place. She shuddered as the implications of *that* little disaster filled her head. Reluctantly, she put the bag on the floor and opened it. She really didn't want to go through it. She wanted nothing to do with anything that might drag her back in to this. It was hard enough trying to step away without the guilt of abandoning Evie.

With her hand poised to slip in between the edges of the zipper, Claire hesitated. There was no way of knowing what was inside, and just sticking her hand in might not be the most sensible thing. She pulled the edges open and peered in first, but everything was a muddle, mostly of paper. She lifted the bag by its ends, turned it upside-down, and shook everything out onto the floor.

It was a jumble; several tightly bundled fabric somethings, a towel, some old newspapers, a document wallet, a bag from a fast food outlet (and a stale greasy smell that suggested it had been there for a while), one reasonably innocuous trainer and a tube of tennis balls. The tube was still sealed, so that went straight back into the bag, as did the trainer once it had been inverted and shaken. The fast food wrapper contained nothing more than the detritus of a meal and she put it to the side – that would need to go into the bin outside as she wouldn't have it stinking up her room all night. The newspapers were from the Real and were three months old. Claire flicked through them, but there seemed to be nothing of obvious interest in them. She put them aside also, to go into the recycling box later.

That left the papers and the two fabric lumps. She hoped it was a tee, but just to be safe she pinched it with finger and thumb to lift it. The garment was wrapped around something and as it rose into the air it started to unroll. Before she could get her other hand around to catch it, the something fell loudly to the floor. Claire froze, screwed her face up, and waited. A moment later her mother was shouting up the stairs.

'Everything OK, poppet?'

'Fine, Mum. Dropped a book. Sorry.'

'A book? Try something lighter,' and, still laughing at her own joke, her mother faded away into the background noise from the TV downstairs.

The something that had fallen to the floor was a little larger than a smartphone and there was a hint of a button on the side. Claire had a horrible feeling that it was from Underland. One of the first things Evie had told her was that bringing tech up was a major no-no. It seemed that even when she wasn't trying, she was managing to dig herself an ever deeper hole with the SFU. Then she remembered she didn't really care.

Not knowing if the object had been wrapped in the tee to protect it or to prevent it from being touched, Claire used the shirt as a glove to turn it over. It had been face down. Along one edge, which she assumed was the top, were the letters 'LMFDA-Mk 4A'. Below that was a transparent window with a needle inside over a series of scales. Across the middle was a sliding switch, with positions labelled from 'x.01' to 'x100', so it was obviously meant to measure something. What that might be, Claire had no idea. The fingers of her right hand wiggled as she toyed with the idea of pushing the button to see what would happen, but then she resolutely rolled the meter up in the tee-shirt and put it to the side. No point tempting fate.

She was more careful with the other bundle and unwrapped it rather than letting it unroll. The contents were just as much contraband, though much more familiar. Even so, Claire used the wrapping to pick up and examine what appeared to be a perfectly normal, if old, pair of Warrior goggles. She re-wrapped them and put them on her bed.

Now all that was left were the papers and the document wallet, which was stuffed full and was held closed by an elastic band. Claire weighed it in her hands and debated if she even wanted to open it. It looked like there were pages and pages and

157

it could be personal stuff she had no right sticking her nose in. If she started, she would have to look at everything. She stalled, taking the stinky food bag down to the bin and making herself a mug of blackberry and nettle tea on the way back.

The folder was still there, and the decision no different. Grimacing, she picked the folder up from the floor and took it over to her bed. There was no way she was going to trawl through it on her knees. The elastic band felt gritty and snapped as she tried to ease it off. Peering under the flap, Claire saw a confusion of paper and she sighed. This was going to take a while.

The paperwork fell into three groups; there were sheets that were maps, sheets that looked like official reports, and lots and lots of notes scrawled on various sizes of paper. Claire sorted them into three piles and used spring-clips to hold them together. The reports and the notes looked dry and boring, so she put them aside in favour of the maps.

Tiredness washed over her, and she started to think it was time to turn in. Being stressed out had made her restless, and it seemed stupid to ignore feeling sleepy. Maybe she could catch up a bit and not feel so beaten in class. As she tried to make up her mind if bed was the best option, Claire browsed through the sheets of map she had clipped together. Some were pristine, whilst others had marks or on them. She stopped, frowned, and turned back a few pages. The frown deepened as she flicked back and forth, then her eyes opened wide and any thoughts of an early night disappeared. All the separate sheets were one big map. It was a jigsaw.

She started to lay the pieces out on the floor, grouping them into areas she knew and others she didn't before starting to line the edges up. It got more complicated as the sheets left were of places she didn't know and before long she was hunting for matching street names along the edges. A few places had missing pages, which cost her time to check and recheck that she hadn't overlooked a match. It took hours to finish. Her parents had already gone to bed, her mother calling a caution through the door that she wasn't to stay up too late. When she was done, Claire stood over it, and had to admit it made no sense at all.

After school the next day, Claire tried to run straight up to her room. Her mother intercepted her in the kitchen. 'Father and I are going out tonight. Will you fix yourself something, or shall I cook and you can reheat it.'

Claire tried to process the utterly random thought, switching her mind away from the map. School had been a major inconvenience. She had tried to be attentive and to push the image of the map out of her head, but it was difficult not to speculate about symbols drawn over much of it. She took the berry tea her mother offered her and slowly turned the mug around and around.

'You'll spill that,' said her mother, making Claire's head jerk up. 'Now, what about the food?'

'I'll do a sandwich, or something,' said Claire, hoping that was an end to the conversation and shifting her weight ready to slide off the breakfast stool. Her mother wasn't finished.

'I nearly tripped over that thing on your bedroom floor this morning.'

Claire struggled not to gasp. 'You didn't tear it or anything, did you?'

'No, I managed to keep to my feet and wasn't hurt thank you. What is it, anyway?'

Claire's mind raced around for a plausible lie before she realised she had a perfectly plausible truth. 'It's a map, of London.' And that was the point she realised the truth wasn't big enough. 'It's for a new game.'

'Well, you need to find somewhere more sensible to put it. Under your bed, if you have to keep it flat?'

'Good idea, Mum. Thanks.' This time her getaway worked and she hurried up to her room. She knelt on the floor and studied the map, trying to see a pattern to the symbols, or their location, and rose only when both her her legs cramped at the same time. Still nothing made sense.

Her parents called out that they were leaving, and she yelled

159

back a barely coherent farewell. She also realised she was hungry, and that now would be a good time to fix something to eat. As has she headed down to the kitchen she picked up the folder of paperwork almost as an afterthought.

The folder, together with a glass of milk and two generously cut cheese and tomato sandwiches, ended up on the kitchen table. As she munched, she pulled the folder closer, opened it, and took out the major bundle of papers. Everything else was loose fragments. Briefly relinquishing the sandwich, she pulled the clip off the top and started leafing through the sheets. They still looked like some stuffy report, but they were uneven, and the print was crooked. Whoever had copied them had been very sloppy, or in a hurry. Quality aside, everything was numbers or abbreviations. The only thing she came close to recognising was 'LMFD', and that was only because mostly the same sequence appeared on the device currently hiding in a drawer, beneath her clean panties.

Claire sighed and picked up the reports before shuffling them into a neat stack and clipping them together again. Evie had gone out of her way to hide this collection of the strange, bizarre, and utterly boring. It must have meant something to her. Enough for her to want to keep it safe, anyway. Or was she, Claire, getting everything completely turned around. Maybe this was just a bag of junk that Evie had been meaning to get rid of, but hadn't actually got around to throwing out yet. She picked up the folder and was about to slip the reports back in when she saw the loose sheets she hadn't looked through yet.

Tilting the folder, Claire let them sigh onto the table. Every scrap seemed to have something of Evie's handwriting on it. Interest re-ignited, Claire turning the pieces face up and laid them out neatly before putting her elbows on the table and her chin in her hands as she scanned across the last of the haul.

Five minutes later, Claire was scowling again and muttering curses under her breath about Evie wasting her time and being awkward, obnoxious and obstructive. Nothing stood out and nothing made any sense. She saw lists of numbers that looked as though they might have been taken from the reports, but everything else was either in code, or shorthand. Nothing seemed to match up with the symbols on the map. Suddenly furious, Claire started picking up the scattered notes and sticking them on top of the reports. She wasn't even going to bother taking them back to her room. They were going straight to the recycling bin and that would be an end to it. The map she could bring down later.

Something felt wrong in her fingers. At first it seemed to be a compliments slip, but as she looked closer it resolved into a long envelope. The flap tucked in rather than glued down, so she flipped it open, cupped her hand beneath the flap, and gently squeezed the sides. A single sheet of folded paper slid out. She put the envelope on the pile to be discarded and opened out the paper, thinking to glance over it before it, too, was consigned to the waste.

Except there were words. Whole words. And recognisable dates. And the words were street names. Some she even recognised, and there were numbers that referred back to the pages of the report. Claire grabbed all the notes from the kitchen table and made for the map. She was still cross-referencing pages when her parents got home. Her mother spoke sharply to her, reminding her that tomorrow was a school day and she needed her sleep. Claire was contrite and agreed she should go to bed, which is where she was when her mother checked on her a quarter of an hour later. School, though, was not on Claire's agenda.

TWENTY TWO

Enough of the weak morning light crept through the window for Claire to get what she needed from the wardrobe. A few minutes later she was suitably attired in Warrior-chic, armed, and feeling terrified by the thought of having no Kevlar. But then, nobody else knew and so long as she acted the part, nobody need find out. She stood straight, pulled her shoulders back, and strode purposefully out of the room.

There had been a few hours sleep the night before, but not many. With the last list she had found in Evie's notes, things had started making sense. Each mark on the map corresponded to a line in the list. The dates went back a year, and seemed to be days where there had been an incursion. Claire remembered two of the dates because she had been personally involved, so she assumed the others were the same.

The incursions tended to cluster around a dozen specific areas, but were several months apart in each cluster. Almost every incursion linked to at least one page of the incomprehensible report. A half-dozen didn't, but Evie had written some numbers against those herself. It still made as much sense as algebra to a hamster.

The list changed at the bottom of the page. Here there were

eight addresses, with no dates or other notes. Four had been crossed out in no apparent order and they made up a second set of symbols on the map. Claire guessed Evie had been visiting the places on that list. Maybe she had gone missing while she was visiting one of the four that weren't crossed out.

Claire's first thought had been to take the documents to the council; to get Aslnaff and the police to see that there was something wrong and force them to do something. Then she remembered how dismissive Aslnaff had been. Even with all this evidence, would he change his mind? He didn't seem to be the type who could admit he had made a mistake. There were also the lengths Evie had gone to hide the paperwork. She wanted this information safe. She was protecting it from somebody, or protecting herself from some consequence of owning it. Claire had fallen asleep, still dressed and on top of her quilt, trying to figure out who it might be Evie was hiding it from.

The next morning she woke feeling alert. She had only slept for a few hours but she had actually slept, and felt immensely better for it. Perhaps it had been because she could finally do something for Evie. The decision she was going to jump into Underland and explore was already made. She figured she could do a few hours, snap back, and get ready for school and still be about as alert as she had been yesterday. A model knife had quickly released the map pages she needed, and she had jotted the four addresses on the back of one before folding them into a pocket.

Now she was walking past a surprised Hrund guarding the bottom of the main staircase in the lobby of the hive, then out the door at the corner of the building. She had checked the map before she jumped in, so she strode off down the street with confidence. Time usually matched between the Real and Underland, at least after jumping in, so it was still early and the streets were quiet and unhurried. A steam-tram puffed and hissed past her heading towards Old St, but most of the traffic was hand carts and pedestrians. The air smelt crisper than usual, as though it hadn't been used too much yet, and the sky was almost white. Nobody seemed interested in Claire, or what she was doing, which suited her perfectly.

The first address was 17 Hoxton Rd, and was a total bust. She scoped around outside, and even bullied her way past the doorman to check out the basement, but the trail was old and useless. She checked her watch. That waste of time had cost her an hour and had been so frustrating that she toyed with the idea of jumping out and going to school. She pulled the list out of her pocket, caught her bottom lip between her teeth, and changed her plans.

The station could not have looked more different than it had on her first visit to Underland. People bustled in and out through the ticket halls, and there was a rumble of noise drifting up from the bottom of the escalators that hinted of rushing trains and passengers brushing past each other as they made their way through the station. Claire hesitated at the top of the escalators, standing between two of them and trying to keep out of peoples' way. She needed some time before she could face going down.

It surprised her how strong and fresh the memories were as they flooded back to her. Fear was trying to tie a knot in her gut and made her breathe in short, shallow gasps. That left her feeling dizzy and added to her growing panic. She closed her eyes and forced her breathing into a slower, deeper rhythm. Moments later, her heart stopped feeling as though it was either going to jump from her throat or straight out of her chest and she could finally step across onto the 'down' escalator.

At the bottom, she stood in the middle of the small hall and held the goggles over her eyes. She heard mumbling and muttered complaints as people gave her a wide berth and the crowd eddied around her. She ignored them and turned in a slow circle. The only traces of Morph activity she could see were vague hints from when she had stumbled accidentally into Underland, and that made no sense. She took off the goggles and walked out onto the platform. Why had Evie been interested in the place if nothing had happened there for so long. When she pushed the goggles over her eyes again to check the platform and to look out along the tunnel, they showed the same story. It made very little sense.

'Oy.' The voice was nasal and irate. Claire turned and found herself confronted by a Grenlick, short even by their standards, wearing a scruffy uniform and looking up at her with more than enough attitude to make up for his stature. 'What do you think you're doing?'

'SFU business,' Claire replied, loftily, for want of anything better to say.

'Well stop it. You're disturbing the passengers.'

'What?'

'People don't like you lot poking around. Makes them think there's something going on. Makes them nervous.' Claire looked down the platform. Apart from a few curious glances, nobody was paying any attention to them at all now, and those that were looking seemed more interested in the Grenlick.

'I'll be as discrete as I can,' said Claire.

'I'll make a complaint if I have to,' said the Grenlick, but Claire had taken the wind out of him when she hadn't got into an argument. He turned and started to walk away, but then looked back over his shoulder. 'I'll be watching.'

'Two minutes,' said Claire, smiling back at him.

He walked off, casting occasional glances over his shoulder. Claire stood where she was; watching, smiling whenever he turned back, then slowly edged her way to the end of the platform. A train thundered past her, squealing to a halt, and as soon as travellers started to disgorge from the doors, Claire spun on her heel and hurried up the rickety ledge along the side of the tunnel.

It was easier, in the sense that this time there was no slime under her feet, but her eyes seemed to take ages to adjust from the bright light of the platform to the gloom of the tunnel. Things felt familiar, faded memories from when she had first come here to rescue Evie, but there was little detail. She forgot about the steps that led from the ledge to the door and stumbled awkwardly down them, twisting an ankle.

The door was still ajar, but only just and an ordinary push didn't move it an inch. The train in the station had already rumbled off, and Claire could see the light of the next train drawing closer. Her head knew so long as she stayed close to the wall she would be all right, but her heart made her push frantically at the stiff door, wanting to be inside before the next train went past.

She stepped over the threshold as the train thundered by and felt the wind tug at the back of her coat. It was probably nowhere near as close as it felt, but she wasn't really interested in any more detail. She fumbled the torch out of her pocket and played the disc of light up and down the walls until she found a light switch, then pulled her goggles over her eyes and started to follow the almost invisible trail.

The maze of corridors was just as confusing and the air still tasted coppery and reminded her of blood. Claire doubted she would have been able to remember the way without the trail, but the brick wall that blocked her path didn't look right. The slime trail turned sharp left and disappeared into the wall.

She stepped back and took the goggles off. Pulling at her bottom lip, Claire struggled with her memory. She was sure that this was where the rough, oval tunnel had branched off from the more business-like ones. And that was why the wall looked wrong. All the other walls were big bricks. 'Breeze blocks', her father called them, and they all had that look as though they had been painted over with really thick paint. But this wall was made of ordinary red bricks, like in a house, and they weren't painted. In fact, they looked rough, and hurried, and there were splops of mortar dotted on the floor. Although she would never have attempted to pass herself off as any kind of builder, or even knowing anything about DIY, Claire got the feeling that the wall had been built from the other side.

'Oy!'

Claire groaned. It was louder, and even more irate, but

unmistakably the voice of the Grenlick official from the platform.

'What do you think you're playing at? We've got trains stopped, we have, while you're mucking about down here. This is a safety issue. You can't just come running around down here, private areas and down tunnels, without proper authorisation and an escort.' He had scuttled up to her, wagging a finger comically in front of her to make his points, and he stopped directly in front of her, no more than two feet away. Only then did his rant cut abruptly off, as though he was drawing breath, as his eyes slid to the left, followed by the rest of his head, when he saw the wall.

'What the bloody hell is that?' He stepped over to the wall, ran his hands over it, then turned them over to look at the red dust on them from the bricks. A hand curled into a pointing finger and he turned back to Clair, jabbing accusingly. 'What have you been up to down here? There's no authorisation for this. I don't care if you're SFU or SFA, you can't go building walls down here. I'll have your number off you, and I want you back up in my office so I can report this t-'

Claire wrapped the essence of her bedroom around her and jumped out, then groaned when she remembered she was still carrying a half dozen items of contraband from Underland. She quickly stripped off, jammed as much of the gear as she could into Evie's bag, and hid it in her wardrobe before running off to shower before school.

TWENTY THREE

Her mother took one look at Claire and put out an arm to stop her as she tried to breeze past. She laid her hand on Claire's forehead, and looked concerned. 'What have you been doing to yourself?' she muttered softly. 'The bags under your eyes are darker than mine.'

Claire smiled, or tried to. She could feel it looked wrong by the way her face moved. 'I'm OK. I'm just tired.'

'Playing that game too long last night?'

Claire started to deny it then nodded; it was a more convenient excuse than trying to make one up.

'Maybe you should think about having a hot soak after dinner and going straight to bed? I know this goes against every instinct in your rebellious teen soul, but it might perk you up.'

Claire nodded. 'I'll think about it.' Her mother looked into her eyes once more, and Claire had to look away. It wasn't often her Mum focused on the moment, but right then Claire could see so much in her eyes she wasn't sure how to deal with it. Her mum gave her a push on the shoulder to send her on her way and Claire went up to her room. Her school bag got dropped under her desk and Claire collapsed onto the bed. Perhaps her mother was right. How much use would she be to Evie if she was stumbling around half asleep?

She groaned, rolled to the edge of the bed and sat up. She had a trail to follow, and there wasn't much time. She would have to go back in after she had eaten. She changed out of her school clothes and into sweat pants and a tee before going down to sit in front of the TV. Could she keep herself awake watching that?

He mother woke her an hour later for dinner; pasta with grilled vegetables in a tomato sauce, delicious and filling. Claire zombied through the food then went to her room, ready to visit the next address. She sat on the side of her bed, leaning over to pull on a pair of socks, and a wave of dizziness swept over her. He stomach heaved and she sat up, making the dizzy turn into full blown head-rush. She froze, waited until either everything settled down or she had to dive for the waste bin. She still felt clammy and although the nausea teased at the bottom of her throat it didn't seem inclined to go further. She rolled onto her side and pushed herself up to the pillow. It might be best to stay down for a while until whatever it was had settled.

When she woke, it was dark. Stifling a groan she grabbed for her alarm clock: 04:55. A light coverlet had been thrown over her, so one of her parents must have checked on her at some point. She pushed it aside and sat up. She felt better; hungry and wide awake. Could she jump into Underland now? It would still be just as dark there. A better plan came to her and she snuck down to the kitchen. Half an hour later she had taken a silent breakfast and had made herself up some sandwiches. She carried them back up to her room, crept about getting dressed and collecting all her gear, then as dawn started to tint the sky grey, she jumped.

Evie's room was almost pitch dark, but Claire could make out just enough to see where the door was. There was nothing she wanted from the room today, so she simply walked out and made her way to the Hive's entrance hall. Two Grenlix were guarding the door inside. The younger of the two looked at her with unashamed curiosity, but the older was outraged. 'The doors are closed. They open at first light.'

170

'I need to leave now,' said Claire.

'The doors are closed. Humans should not be here. No good Grenlick would try—'

'I'm here with the Hivemaster's consent,' Claire said, stretching the truth a little, and stretching herself up to her full height. She wondered if that trick worked against a people who were pretty much shorter than everybody else anyway. 'Now if you don't open the door, I will.'

'Unacceptable.'

'And you plan to stop me how?' Claire gambled again. She knew they couldn't bear to touch her, and they didn't know she wasn't wearing a Kevlar. Or she hoped they didn't. Either way, she locked eyes with the older Grenlick and refused to back down. Eventually, he lowered his eyes and made a gesture to the youngster, and together they turned and lifted the solid beam from across the doors. 'Thank you,' said Claire, as a bolt was pulled and a small door creaked open inside the larger frame of the main door.

'I shall speak to the Hivemaster of this, Human. If you live in our dwelling, it is only right that you respect our ways. There is no respect in this.'

Claire, who had stepped out onto the street, turned back to apologise and explain, but the door was already closed behind her. She shrugged and marched away. The Grenlick had a point. As she walked, she dug the square of map out of her pocket. She hadn't really had time to plan a route from the hive to the next location on Evie's list, but it looked like a good thirty minute walk. She checked her watch, and looked up at the sky. There was already a vague sense that sunrise – or what passed for it here – wasn't far off.

It was more like forty minutes than thirty, and when she got there the place looked like a building site. An eight foot high wall of cheap board had been put up around the perimeter, hiding the first floor of a three storey building. There was no guard but the double wooden gates were heavily chained. Claire thought about waiting, then remembered that kids always seemed to find a way in to every building site and decided to take a walk around the perimeter.

The next building along had a low, decorative wall with railings all along the front; almost as good as a ladder. Claire climbed up and looked into the building site. All the windows had been boarded over at ground level and she couldn't see any doors. Two more rows of windows above were so dark they seemed to suck light out of the air. The eight foot drop on the other side of the fence looked huge to her, and the ground on the other side appeared hard and unforgiving.

She climbed over anyway. There was one scary moment when it felt as though she was going to fall back the wrong way, but she windmilled her arms until she was settled again, then leaned forward and pushed herself well clear of the wall.

It was a hard landing. She hit the ground, rolled to her left and thumped against the side of the building. Her feet stung and she lay there for a moment, catching her breath and gently twisting arms and legs, wrists and ankles, checking that everything felt whole. When everything seemed to be working she clambered to her feet and brushed the dirt off her coat before checking nothing had fallen out of her pockets.

The tall fence kept out enough noise to make the courtyard and island of quiet, and every step she took sounded elephantine. When she saw the wooden gates ahead of her she paused, ducking back around the corner. Ahead was a small courtyard, and she realised she had been wandering about as though she knew there was nobody inside. What if she was being watched? She peeked quickly around the corner, checking to see if there was a guard inside the gates, but the place still looked deserted. Keeping tight to the wall, she turned into the courtyard and made for the doors.

Now she could get a decent look, Claire saw that where there had once been steps had been crushed and made into a slope with hard packed earth. At the top, temporary wooden gates hung from crude hinges hammered brutally into the walls. The pool of unnatural stillness seemed to stifle Claire, and the air felt thick in her throat. She walked up to the gates and felt her forehead crinkle into a frown when she found they were also padlocked.

She checked her watch. 07.30. If anybody was coming to work here, they would be arriving soon. She gave the chain an angry tug. It rattled noisily and Claire froze. It had made far too much noise, but it had moved. Her heart hammered as much from hope as fear. She checked the chain again, looking to see what had caused the movement, and started to grin. Whoever had put the chain on had been careless. A loop nearly a foot long was still hanging behind the gate. As quietly as she could, Claire pulled the slack through until it was all on her side of the gates. Then, biting her lower lip, she eased the left gate open. It pulled towards her with a gentle groan, matched by Claire when she saw how small the gap was. She had made herself a hole less than a foot wide; not enough for her to slip through. She pulled angrily at the door and it wobbled, pivoting around the chain. Claire dropped to her knees. Maybe if she pushed only against the bottom, the gate would swing out a bit more? She ended up lying on the floor and pulling herself through, but she made it inside, and felt very pleased with herself.

The board over the windows made the ground floor as dark as night, so Claire pulled the torch out of her pocket and switched it on. The light from the beam seemed weaker than usual, and more yellow, but Claire passed it off as being an optical effect. After all, Evie had told her that the torch never ran out. Dim torch or not, there was no hiding the chasm in the middle of the floor.

TWENTY FOUR

It was a hole with a purpose. A ramp at least four yards wide sloped down into it from right inside the door and Claire followed it with the beam of her torch. It went almost to the limit of the beam then curved to the left. Heavy wooden trusses supported the roof, and there were wheel tracks in the dust.

Light shone down a flight of stairs on the far side of the room and seemed to beckon her away from the ramp. She slid the goggles over her eyes to check if there was any nearby Morph activity. A blur of old trails led down the ramp and several more, fresher but still weeks old, were on the stairs. They all merged into a third broad trail heading out the doors.

Claire didn't spend a lot of time considering options. She wasn't going down that hole unless she had to, which meant she had to explore upstairs first. The short stretch where the tunnel burrowed under the foot of the stairs made her nervous and she hopped quickly across as she pattered up the first flight.

At the first landing corridors stretched off to left and right, a dozen or so doors opening off each side. Some were open and they, plus the big windows at either end of the corridors, were where the light was coming from. Claire pulled a wry face. If she had to check each room, she would be here until tomorrow.

She decided to follow the Morph trails first, and they mostly turned left at the landing. There was one very old trace that carried on up to the next floor, but it wasn't bright enough to tempt her to follow it, so she walked along the corridor and around a corner at the far end. All the doors were closed here and it grew dim again. Claire swept the beam of the torch around but it seemed even fainter and yellower than before. Just as she saw the Morph trail disappear under a door, the torch faded to nothing.

Claire switched the torch on and off a few times, slapping it against her palm for good measure, but bulb remained stubbornly dark. If Evie hadn't already told her it worked on magic, Claire would have said the batteries had run flat. She put the useless thing in her pocket. At least her goggles still showed her the shining trail, and even a dab of brightness where the handle was.

Cracking the door open an inch Claire waited, counting heartbeats hammering in her ears and trying to listen past them for any sounds inside. She eased the door open, peering through the widening gap and ready to slam it and run if there was anything inside. Gritty light fought its way through dirty windows into a big room that looked like it was being used as a store. Claire pushed her goggles up and took a few cautious steps inside. Wooden crates and cardboard boxes were scattered haphazardly about, some open, and some empty or spilled. Dust hung heavy in the air, sparkling in the light and tickling her nose.

There was something about the disorder that looked unintentional. Claire pulled the goggles over her eyes again and gasped. The room was covered with silver confusion. It shone from just about everywhere on the floor, from most of the boxes and crates, and there were even spatters over the walls. Great violence had happened here. She turned a slow circle, trying to make sense of the mess, and gradually the spatter patterns resolved themselves into two loci, each marking the violent end of a Morph.

So much of the floor was covered with silver that it was impossible to make anything out from trails. She pulled her goggles down and let them dangle around her neck while she turned another circle. As her line of sight changed the mess of boxes resolved into a visual line, and at the end of the line were two dents in the wall.

The plaster had fallen away and cracked lathes stuck out like broken bones. Something hard and heavy had been thrown against the wall, and Claire remembered the tonguefist attacks Morph used. As she walked towards the wall she saw two more of the dents, this time in the side of a wooden crate, and scrapes in the dust of the floor where the crate had been shoved aside.

'Oh, you idiot,' Claire muttered, realising she was treading over tracks that might be useful. She stopped and squatted down for a better look at what was ahead of her. There were a couple of shapes that could have been shoeprints, but they were almost brushed out by some twisting marks that swept behind a crate. The pattern disappeared behind a crate that had fallen from atop another. She moved carefully forward until she could see behind it, but froze and looked sharply over her shoulder.

Had that been a sound? She kept as still as she could, holding her breath and waiting to hear the noise again. Everything was quiet apart from the faintest murmur of city life outside. She let the breath out through puffed cheeks and was about to turn back when she saw she had made the same twisting, serpentine marks in the dust. It was her coat dragging on the floor. Her heart quickened. Had another Warrior been here?

The dust behind the crate was disturbed in swirls, but no marks led away. Claire let her eyes follow the imaginary line she had seen to the next box. There was a huge dust-free square in front of it as though it had been pushed aside. As she got closer, she changed her mind. There was a crack in the lid of the box, near an edge that would have been near the top if it had been facing the Morphs. It wasn't pushed, it had been knocked over.

She stepped around the side of the box and drew in a sharp breath, her hands coming up to cover her mouth. On the other

177

side of the box was a large smudge in the dust, then a long scraping slide. And on the wall, a foot above the floor, was a dark smear. Claire rushed over and looked at the smudge, cursing her torch as she tried to see what colour it was. Hesitantly, she touched it; bone dry and barely registering under her fingers. Even though it looked black, it had to be blood.

Standing up and turning back to face the door, she closed her eyes and a vision of what could have happened played out in her mind. Evie running into the room, already being chased. Taking cover behind the two stacked boxes. Waiting until the Morphs followed her into the room. There had to be at least three, perhaps four. Taking a shot, bursting one. A barrage of fists, two missing, hitting the wall, one eventually hitting the top box Evie was hiding behind. A second shot, and another Morph disposed of, but then a strike, probably to her body, absorbed by her Kevlar but throwing her backwards into the other box and toppling it over. It would have hurt, a lot, but Evie wouldn't have given up. She maybe took out one more Morph, but there was no third explosion of silver. Then a last strike, the fist smashing into her, sliding her along the floor and crashing her head into the wall. Why hadn't her Kevlar protected her?

Claire opened her eyes and took a deep breath. Her eyes pricked with moisture. Evie had been taken by Morphs. Again. She shied away from the other option, making the excuse that there wasn't enough blood. Her eyes cast around, looking for Evie's PPG. There had to be a reason she hadn't taken out a third Morph, and it could be because she had lost her grip on the gun. Claire saw no gun but a faint sparkle caught at her eye, far outside the line where everything had happened. She almost ignored it, but that something could shine on this otherwise dusty floor pricked at her curiosity.

It wasn't until she picked it up she realised what it was. Dangling from her fingers by a broken cord, totally exhausted, was a Kevlar amulet. Trembling, she turned it over and checked the number. 6412. Evie's.

TWENTY FIVE

Claire tucked the Kevlar away in an inside pocket. She was beginning to understand why the tracks were so wide; several Morphs had followed each other. So did that mean the important track was the one going out of the building, or the one going down into the pit? She took a last look around the room, just to make sure she hadn't missed anything, then retraced her steps to the bottom of the stairs. It was difficult to be sure, but it still looked as though the strongest trails went out through the gates. She made a decision, and headed out of the building.

A crate against the side fence made for a convenient exit. The street was busier now, and several people stopped to watch her. She ignored them, and pulled her goggles over her eyes as she made her way back to the gate.

The trail went back down St Martin's Street. Claire kept her head down, focusing on the trail and expecting everybody else to exercise good sense and get out of her way. She heard a few muttered curses, but nobody bumped into her as she walked along.

She had no idea where she was or where she was going, but the longer the chase went on, the more uneasy Claire became. She had never followed a trail for this long before. Then doubts started to creep in. What if she had taken a wrong turn? There had been two places where she had hesitated, not sure of the right path. Could she have missed it then? Should she go back?

The trail opened out onto a major road and Claire was shocked by how busy it was. Nose to tail carriages trundled slowly by in four lanes, horns braying irritably at each other. She lurched to a stop in the middle of the pavement, people of all races frantically dodging to keep from touching her, the effect rippling outwards along the sidewalk. A quick glance at her watch confirmed she was in the middle of rush hour.

The trail went diagonally across the road, which Claire belatedly recognised was Piccadilly - or as close as this world came to it. She darted between two steam trams and ran across to the other pavement. The trail ran on ahead of her, passing across the front of an imposing building, then turned down a side road. She hurried after it, figuring she might as well see this trail to the end before she worried about whether she had missed a turn.

The building looked like a palace. Tall iron railings, with equally imposing gates, protected a wide crescent drive and port-cochere from the street. There were Hrund at either gate and at the door, dressed in black uniforms and looking impassive and imposing. Claire found herself picking up her pace as she passed. Something about the scrutiny of the Hrund guards made her feel uncomfortable, and she could feel eyes boring into her back as she turned down the side road.

Albany, which seemed to be all the name the alley had, slid along the side of the courtyard and palace. She could see another street at the far end, but the trail seemed to turn to the left before it got there. She took off her goggles and tried to look as though she was just strolling past.

Where the trail turned left, a ramp dropped down under the wall and ended in two metal gates. It looked like a delivery entrance, and the two Hrund guarding it took an immediate interest in her as she passed. Claire tried to keep her look casual, nodding and offering a neutral smile to the Hrund as she walked

180

past the top of the ramp and on out to Vigo Street.

Her knees were trembling. She really needed to find somewhere to sit down and settle herself. Something was screaming to her that Evie was inside, and something else was telling her that his time she couldn't bully her way in. From the looks the Hrund had given her she wouldn't even get close to them, let alone past them and into the building. She stopped and leaned against a wall, scratching her scalp vigorously with her fingernails in the vain hopes of waking up her mind. There was no escaping it; she was going to need help.

Broad Street Airship Terminus was still busy with the morning rush. The roof doors were permanently open for ships to land and depart, and Claire could see more ships circling the station overhead as they waited for the opportunity to disgorge their passengers. She was sitting outside a small snack food bar in a quiet corner of the concourse, facing out so she could watch the bustle. And look for Jack.

He had been the 'help' she had thought of as soon as she realised she was out of her depth, and she had called him as soon as she had been able to stop her hands shaking enough to hold the phone-thing. He hadn't seemed pleased to hear from her, and had rushed through the conversation as though he was trying to get rid of her. The location had been all cryptic hints, and even now she hoped she had got it right. He was ten minutes late.

Then she saw him, striding across the concourse, and had to resist the urge to stand up and wave. He walked nervously, quickly, looking around too much. She was sure he had seen her, but it looked like he was going to walk straight past until he made a sudden turn and walked up to the café. 'Hi,' said Claire, but the rest of what she had been going to say died in her throat, as did the idea they might hug, or even kiss. He looked furious.

'What the hell are you playing at?'

'Pardon?'

'Using a communicator. Those things can be monitored, tracked.'

'I didn't know,' said Claire, her eyes dropping from his face

181

and her cheeks starting to burn. 'How else was I supposed to get in touch with you? It's not like we ever exchanged mobile numbers or anything.' Claire felt herself starting to get as angry as Jack looked and forced herself to calm down. 'All right, I'm sorry and I obviously shouldn't have done it that way, but I needed to talk to you.'

'What about? You do know you shouldn't be here, don't you? Everybody got the memo that you'd been suspended. Nobody in the SFU is going to help you. They won't want to get into trouble.'

'Does that include you?'

The silence stretched out way too far. 'What did you want to see me about?' Jack said, eventually.

Claire told him most of what she had found out over the last week. Most. She didn't tell him about the gadget, or the copied reports. If anybody had asked her, she wouldn't have been absolutely sure why. Jack didn't interrupt until she mentioned the exhausted Kevlar.

'It must be broken,' he said. 'It would have recharged.'

'That's what I thought, too,' said Claire. 'It must have been some fight to hit it hard enough to break it.'

And the story went on. When she got to the end, Jack looked pale. 'At least you had the good sense not to try to get in there.'

'Why?' said Claire, heart sinking as she realised Jack's concerned face was not for Evie but for her, and for this palace.

'That's the Stellar Cellar. It's one of the most exclusive nightclubs in Underland London.'

'So?'

Jack rolled his eyes. 'All nightclubs are run by Angels, at least all the top ones, and they are all bent. They run all kinds of nastiness out of them, and the Stellar is run by Natrak Sum. He's bad, even for an Angel.'

Claire felt she ought to remember the name, but it butterflied around the edges of her memory and wouldn't make a connection. 'So what do you think?'

'About what?'

'Everything,' she said, frowning. 'What I just told you. You were listening?'

'I was, but it doesn't really change anything.'

'What? Why not?'

'No evidence.'

Claire opened her mouth to argue, but had to admit he was right. Everything she had discovered, she had been the only person there, and even then all she had was a gut feeling. It was all nothing more than her word. Almost. She reached into an inside pocket. 'Really? What about this?' and she slapped the amulet down on the table.

With a curse, Jack leaned forward and covered it with his hand, then his brow furrowed and he picked the amulet up. 'I thought you said it was drained.'

'It is.'

'Was, maybe, but it's fine now,' he replied, turning it around so Claire could see the red gem on the front. It glowed healthily, and showed full charge. Claire reached into another pocked, pulled out the torch and, looking down into the bulb, switched it on. She cried out and squeezed her eyes shut as she fumbled to switch it off, and when she opened her eyes a wide purple streak overlaid everything. She could make out that Jack was looking at her like she was an idiot. 'It went flat,' she explained. 'In the house. It died like the battery had gone flat.'

'But it's recharged, automatically, from the standing magical field–' Jack started.

'I know that, but it still stopped working,' Claire snapped.

'How long were you using it?'

'Only ten minutes.'

'Could be faulty.'

Claire ignored him, thinking hard on something else.

'Jack, what would a LMDFA measure?'

'LM eff dee A,' he corrected. 'Local Magical Field Density Analyser...' His voice died away as he spoke and more ridges appeared on his brow. Claire told him the last details. Holding back wouldn't help Evie if it meant she couldn't get any help. 'I suppose it's possible,' he said when she had finished. 'Although it would be really, really unlikely to find a field density that low. But why would Jones be going around looking at places with a poor local field? Just to see if she could drain magical devices?'

'Help me get her out and we can ask her,' Claire said. Jack scowled at her, but she smiled sweetly at him and waited. Eventually, he gave in.

'It's near impossible,' he said. 'You do know that, don't you? Getting into Stellar Cellar without an invite or a membership.'

'There must be a way. Isn't there anybody who will help us?'

'Not officially. You need something like a tame Grenlick. They're all crooks. That's their speciality; stealth and subterfuge. That might get you something useful.'

'Any other ideas?'

Jack shrugged. 'Not really. I can start checking a few things out. See if maybe I can get some building plans, or some inside stuff on the Cellar.'

'How long?'

'No idea. How long have you been here?'

Claire checked her watch it was showing a few minutes before ten. 'About five hours.'

'You should snap back. Wait around until about five, local time, then jump back in and meet me here. Just watch out for the commuters.' He got up and threw some coins down on the table. Slightly annoyed he had decided the conversation was finished all on his own, Claire got up too. Jack hesitated, fidgeted from foot to foot for a moment, then he gave her a clumsy wave and walked off. Claire waited until he was out of sight, wondering what it was Jack had been trying to get the nerve to do, then walked off in the opposite direction. She still had some work to do.

Turner's Road was becoming familiar ground to Claire now, and she moved confidently down Cotton St to the shop run by Krennet Tolks. For a change, the door was open and there was a great bustling in and out. Claire recognised at least two of Tolks' apprentices, but the rest were strangers to her. There was a van

184

parked outside, hissing softly and venting a thin streamer of steam. Large objects were being carried out of the shop and into the van, all carefully wrapped in sacking.

Claire held back, watching but trying not to intrude. Whatever was going on was no business of hers, and there didn't seem to be any point in making trouble with Tolks by barging in on the situation. Instead, she waited until one of the apprentices looked up and caught her eye. She didn't see any reaction, but a couple of moments later Tolks himself walked out of the shop, casually looking around and supervising the loading. Nobody could have spotted his covert glance at Claire, or the three fingers he held briefly splayed across the side of his trouser leg. Claire levered herself away from the wall and walked off. She had thirty minutes to idle away until Tolks was free to talk to her.

When she got back the street was all but empty and, surprisingly, the door to Tolks shop was unlocked. She let herself in, closed the door behind her, and waited in the outer shop. Instead of the usual clutter, the space was almost empty and sounds seemed to chase around it like bats. When nobody came out to the front of the shop to greet her she tried a quiet 'Hello' that even sounded timid to her.

Still there was no response, so she walked to the back of the shop and tapped lightly at the door that led out to the workshop. It moved, so she pushed it farther open and peered inside. The room was uninhabited, apart from Tolks. He was busy pouring steaming water from a delicate silver kettle into two small cups. A strong aroma of something suspiciously like coffee filled the room. He put the kettle down on a cork coaster and gestured that she should pull one of the other stools over to his bench. Once she was settled, he pushed one of the tiny cups towards her.

'You have news of Warrior Jones?' he asked, lifting his own cup and inhaling deeply before taking a delicate sip. Claire raised her own cup. Coffee wasn't something she drank, but the aroma was wonderful; rich and enticing, bitter and sweet at the same time. She tried a sip, then another. The second made her

185

shudder with the intensity of the flavour, but it wasn't unpleasant. She wasn't she sure about the rush of heat washing out from her core or the noticeable acceleration of her heartbeat. She put the cup down and took a long, slow breath through her nose, the air still redolent with coffee, before she spoke.

'I do. I think she was taken captive by two or more Morphs while she was investigating a building site on Orange St. I think she was looking into dead spots in the magical field, and that was one of them.'

'Do you know where she was taken?'

'I… maybe.'

'You do or you don't. Perhaps you should start from the beginning?'

Claire said nothing for a moment. She was trying to keep her face neutral but think at the same time. Could she trust this Grenlick? Everything she had been taught suggested Grenlix were fickle, but Evie seemed to have faith in this one. And Claire needed help.

'I went to Evie's room at Hive Straknat. She wasn't there, but I found some stuff she had left behind; goggles, this PPG, and a key.'

'May I see that,' Tolks asked, pointing at the PPG. Claire handed it over. Tolks checked the safety then examined the weapon. 'This is old,' he said. 'Mk 18, if I am not mistaken. Six shots in the crystal, two shot fast recharge. Have you tried it?'

Claire shook her head. It hadn't occurred to her to shoot the thing to make sure it worked, and the thought of the gun might be broken made her feel sick – she had been relying on it to 'replace' her Kevlar. Tolks climbed down from his stool, walked across to one of the other benches, and fitted the PPG into a clamp before attaching two devices at the stock and another over the barrel.

A moment later the PPG started to fire. Claire lost count of the number of times oddly constricted clouds of purple spat from then end and, after little more than a minute, Tolks returned to the weapon and unhooked it from the gadgetry.

'The crystal is in good condition, but the emitter is slightly out of focus. The device will serve you for now.'

He held it out to her, but when Claire reached out to take it, her hand touched Tolks. As soon as she sensed the contact she snatched her hand away, almost dropping the weapon. She started a babble of apologies, but Tolks didn't look angry or hurt. He looked thoughtful. Claire let her apologies slow to a trickle and stop. Something had felt odd about the contact. There had been something, but it hadn't been painful – not like when she had touched the policeman. Tolks climbed back onto his stool then gave Claire a very direct look.

'Has anything you have used in Underland done something you didn't expect it to, or that caused others to comment?'

Claire felt her eyebrows rise. What an odd question. What had she used apart from PPG, phone, torch, security pads, and goggles. 'Nothing I can think of. Except when someone loaned me some Observer goggles to look through. He said my eyes hadn't adjusted to them properly.'

'Why?'

'Oh, I saw little red streaks coming down from the sky.'

Tolks shrugged his shoulders and made a nothing sort of noise, but Claire couldn't shake the feeling that something had happened and Tolks wasn't sharing.

'Tell me more about Jones,' he said.

Claire told him the rest of the story. '... and then I followed the trails to a club, called the Stellar Cellar.'

Tolks eyebrows clicked outwards. 'Are you sure?'

'As sure as I can be following a trail two weeks old.'

He grunted and turned his eyes down to his coffee, taking another sip. Claire did the same, liking it even more. When Tolks spoke, his voice was so quiet that Claire had to concentrate to make out the words. 'I knew she was doing the survey, and assumed it wasn't officially sanctioned. Why else would she have come to me for the analyser? But how could she come to be in trouble through it? Who could have any interest in weak areas in the field except the ministry?'

'No idea,' said Claire. 'I mean, why would anybody want to dig a hole in the ground inside a building?'

'A what?' Tolks sat upright and paid much more attention. Claire described the ramp and the curve, and the Grenlick started to stroke the scraggy beard sprouting from his chin. 'There are many reasons someone might dig such a tunnel, and none I can think of are honest. It may be we now know why Warrior Jones was taken.'

'But by Morphs?'

Tolks' mouth twisted. 'You neatly drive a wedge into the weak point of my theory. It is most unfortunate. A Sum is a worthy enemy at the best of times, and Natrak is one of the more ruthless of that caste. Have you told your masters?'

'I don't think they would listen to me. I've been told to stay out of it, and stay out of Underland.'

Tolks chuckled, a curiously gravelly sound. 'You share Jones' disrespect for authority, bureaucracy, and fools. I like that.'

'How much?' said Claire. Looking very directly at him.

'Beg pardon?'

'How much do you like that? Enough to help me get into the nightclub?'

Tolks spluttered for a moment, tried to sip the last of his coffee, and ended up in a coughing fit. 'You have no idea what you are asking.'

'Nope, no idea at all,' Claire agreed, 'but there is no cavalry coming over the hill. I am absolutely sure that Evie is in there, and I know I can't get myself in or her out without some real help. She had nothing but good things to say about you, and I think there is something about her that you like - way more than you're telling me. What I'm asking is how far does that go? I've been told you folk are the best there is at stealth and getting into difficult locations. What can I do to get you to help me?'

Claire flinched back as a strange look flickered across Tolks face, before it settled into a kind, sly good humour. 'I'm sure we can think of something.'

TWENTY SIX

Jack was waiting for her when she jumped back in to Broad Street later that afternoon. Claire had snapped back when she had finished with Tolks and, as it was still before six in the morning, she had crashed and caught a couple of hours of sleep before going to school. The five pm meet had been a challenge. Getting home in time had been a huge rush, as had getting changed and then jumping into Underland. She felt dishevelled, and unprepared.

'What have you found out?' she asked as soon as they were seated.

'Nothing much,' Jack admitted, looking unhappy. 'There's not a lot about the place on file. And nobody seems to know anything about it, either. Just rumours.'

Claire scowled. 'So what can we do? We have to find a way in, or some plans to the building.'

'No chance. The Cellar is a high class affair. Only top people go there; rich, famous, or influential. Makes it easy to keep secrets.'

Claire hesitated, not sure how her next question was going to be received. 'How far will you go? With me? Tonight. I mean breaking in, or whatever.' She felt her face go bright red as she realised she hadn't chosen her words that well. Jack was laughing at her again, but he got it under control quickly. Perhaps he saw that she wasn't amused.

'I don't know,' he said, fighting to control a huge grin. She gave him marks for his honesty if not for his commitment. 'This could get us both in a lot of trouble. The sort you can't get yourself out of. And I'm not even sold Jones is in there. Even if she is, we have no idea where. That place is huge, and we won't be able to search all of it.'

'We may not have to. We can follow the Morph trails.'

'Unless they were just dropping her off.'

Claire had to admit he had a point. There were a lot of unknowns, and she was asking a lot of him. She, on the other hand, hadn't anything to lose.

'Do we know when this place opens?'

'I don't think it ever shuts.'

Claire decided it was time to let Jack in on her latest secret.

'I have some stuff that can help us.'

'Like what?'

'I have a friend. A Grenlick. He gave me some gadgets. I have three things he called 'distractors', and an amulet that can make you invisible.'

'You're kidding.'

'Honest. He said two of the 'distractors' were subtle, and the other wasn't.'

'And the invisibility? What did he tell you about that?' There was a note of disbelief in Jack's voice, and Claire pushed back a flash of resentment. It was almost as though he didn't trust her, or didn't believe her.

'Well, he said it was for stealth. So long as whoever is wearing it stays out of bright light and doesn't make too much noise it will hide them. He said 'conceal'. Anybody touching the one wearing the amulet is also hidden.'

Jack's face was sceptical, matching his voice. 'I'd like to see that before I trust it.'

'Can't. Once it's activated, it's activated, and it only lasts about two hours. Less if it has to hide more than one person.'

Jack nodded as though he'd been expecting the catch. 'No surprise. Never seems to be quite what you want when you deal with a Grenlick. Whatever you paid for it, I hope it wasn't too much.' He looked very directly at Claire, and she met his eyes. What her agreement had been with Tolks was nothing to do with him.

'I do have an idea,' said Claire. 'It's a bit of a gamble, though.'

'So long as it's not trying to creep past the guards on the front door, I'll listen,' said Jack.

Two hours later Claire was standing in a shadowed doorway on Vigo St, looking down towards the junction with Albury. Jack was similarly tucked away somewhere on Piccadilly.

She tried to make herself invisible, unremarkable, projecting a shell of anonymity around herself. She didn't dare use the amulet yet. Tolks had warned her that they were rare and that he only had the one. Worse still, they didn't recharge on their own, which was a shame because she felt dreadfully exposed and vulnerable where she was. At least she had a Kevlar again. During school she had repaired the broken link on Evie's amulet and it hung reassuringly around her neck, fully charged. There had been a moment, just as she jumped in, when she wondered if Evie's amulet had been booby-trapped, but nothing seemed to be trying to immobilize her, so she guessed not.

It was getting dark. Claire was feeling cold and stiff and wondering if the whole idea was the worst thing she had ever thought of when she heard, rather than saw, a delivery truck lumbering past her. Exactly what she had been waiting for. It clinked and rattled with the clatter of a hundred glass bottles as it slowed and made the turn into Albury. As quickly as she could with fingers slightly numb, Claire used her communicator to call Jack, and then hung up straight away. Without making herself too obvious, she hurried to the corner of Albury to be sure the driver wasn't simply taking a short cut. He wasn't, and she saw

191

him slowing down to take the tight turn down the delivery ramp. She made another call and again hung up straight away. Jack should now have been at the other end of Albury and away from the nightclub.

Claire took a distractor from her pocket. It was the one Tolks had described as not being very subtle. It was a tiny thing, no bigger than the oversized marbles her boy friends used to call '3-ers' in her infancy. She lined her thumbs and forefingers up with the four spots on the outside, took a breath, and squeezed. She felt a click. Sixty seconds before it went off. She rolled the marble along the gutter, down Vigo St and away from the nightclub, then walked towards the ramp.

A countdown ticked in her head. The stealth amulet was already around her neck, outside her clothes as instructed. The amulet was made of two discs, dark as night but with a slight dusting of silver specks across the surface of the front one. She took the two discs, one in each hand, and rotated them against each other, widdershins, until she felt a click. Forty five seconds to go.

A slight mist fogged her sight, like looking through a veil. Not enough to actually stop her seeing anything, but still undeniably there. She walked across the ramp, looking down to see the doors still in the process of being opened, then stood to the side and waited for Jack. Thirty seconds left. She could see him walking towards her, on the correct side of the street. He stopped where he was supposed to, and she had to stifle a giggle at him not being able to see her. She fought down an urge to touch him somewhere he wasn't expecting, like maybe his ear, then made sure nobody was looking before she reached out to take his hand. She felt him flinch, then his hand wrapped around her and squeezed gently. Fifteen seconds.

At five seconds she started to squeeze his hand every second. She miscounted, and the distractor went off with two seconds left. Bedlam erupted from the direction of Vigo St. There was a flash of light and the roar of a huge explosion. People started screaming, and there was the crunch of vehicles colliding. More screaming and a billowing cloud of dust and smoke started to make its way along Albury. Claire had to fight the urge to go and help herself, and she knew it was a trick. Or she hoped it was, and not just a coincidence.

She and Jack edged down the ramp towards the doors. The driver and both guards were Hrund, and the drivers mate looked to be a Sathaari. They were all looking at each other, and up at the apparent disaster. The doors to the underground parking bay were open, but not wide enough for Claire and Jack to edge past the guards. Claire started to silently mouth 'go and help, go and help' over and over as if she could will them to leave.

It was the driver who cracked first. He pushed his assistant in front of him and said 'Let's go,' as he turned to walk up the ramp. When he noticed the guards weren't following him, he turned back. 'There could be people hurt up there.'

'Not our problem,' said one of the guards, but Claire could see in his face that he wasn't happy. The other guard turned to look at him.

'I suppose, if one of us...?'

The first guard looked troubled, then gave a jerky nod. Three of them went up the ramp and headed off along the street while one stayed put. Claire stifled a groan. That wasn't the plan. And he was standing in exactly the wrong place, blocking their path through the gates. As if on cue there was another mighty thump from the end of the street and the sound of falling debris. The remaining guard fidgeted, then walked quickly up the ramp to see what was going on. Claire pulled hard on Jack's arm and they ran forward. They were in.

The underground space was astonishingly big; plenty of room for the delivery van to drive inside and turn around. To one side there was a smarter area, with clean paint on the walls and a piece of red carpet on the floor in front of what looked like the grille for a lift. She wondered what sort of place this was that important people would want to come and go without being seen, then she turned her attention back to business. Awkwardly, with only one hand free, Claire put on her goggles and started tracking the Morph spoor. The agreement was that Jack would be their eyes in the mundane world, and he would keep a watch for her.

The Morphs had gone straight across the loading bay and through a double door on the opposite side. She cursed softly. Doors were a big risk. Even though neither she nor Jack would be noticed, doors opening and closing on their own were a little conspicuous. At least these had windows in them, and she let Jack ease in front of her so he could look through. He pushed the door open after a hurried glance and they darted through.

The trail went straight along the main corridor. Claire had hoped it would disappear off to a quieter part of the basement, but it seemed to be doing the opposite. There were no people near them, but the noise from ahead was getting louder and more distinct, like the clatter of metal on metal with hissing and bubbling overtones. They came up to another set of doors, again with windows, and Jack groaned softly when he looked through.

'What is it?' Claire whispered.

'A kitchen, and it's full of people.'

TWENTY SEVEN

'What?' Claire rose onto tiptoe and tried to peer through the window, almost losing her grip of Jack's hand in the process. The trail went straight through and out a matching set of doors on the other side. 'Can we make our way around the edges?'

'That's where the ovens and stuff are, and there are benches down the middle where food's being prepared.'

That didn't fit with what Claire had seen. 'But I saw the Morph trail, all the way across.'

'Well, there is a gap between the tables, but it's only a couple of feet wide.'

She thumped him with her free arm. 'That's wide enough for us, idiot. So long as nobody else is using it.'

There was a short, relative silence as Jack looked again, then he suddenly flattened back against the wall. 'Someone's coming.'

Claire tugged at his arm and hissed. 'Double idiot. That's what we want. Which side of the door are they headed for?' 'Left. No, right,' said Jack.

'One or the other,' Claire complained, and at that moment Jack pushed her to the right. A second later the left-hand door banged open and a Sathaari with an empty trolley pushed through and down the corridor. The door was already starting to close as Claire pulled Jack through. She heard a thump from the door and he stumbled. Claire guessed he had clipped his heel, and hoped nobody noticed.

The kitchen was a mad clatter of activity, hot and steamy with a deafening, perpetual cacophony of clattering and shouting from one end to the other. Claire couldn't breathe. Had they made a terrible mistake and there was no way they could possibly get across without someone noticing them? She worried about the billowing clouds of steam, too. Would the amulet still hide them, or would the mist eddy around them, and show them up. She pushed the thoughts aside. They were where they were and she had to find a way out of the problem. She hauled Jack back against the wall next to the door while she pulled the goggles around her neck and looked across the kitchen.

'This is hopeless,' Jack said in her ear. It was so noisy he could speak in a normal voice. 'We'll never get through. We have to try to find a way around.'

Claire didn't answer, although the same thing had occurred to her. What she didn't like about the idea was how long it might take them to find a new route, assuming it even existed. The amulet would only last so long. She watched the kitchen, the way it worked, the way the people moved, and tried to filter out Jack's fidgeting. A moment later she tugged on his arm and he leant down to hear her.

'Look. There. See the pattern?'

Jack's eyes followed her pointing finger, and she prayed she wasn't inventing it, finding a pattern where none existed. Between the parallel rows of preparation tables the traffic was much lighter. People doing the preparation worked on the outside. The inside space was only used by helpers bringing things to be worked on. They started at the same end as Claire and Jack, and worked down the aisle before breaking away through a space in the middle. The process repeated for the second row. All they had to do was walk behind one of the assistants as they worked their way down the aisle.

'Might work,' said Jack, 'but if it doesn't, we're screwed.'

Claire saw a Grenlick carrying a half-dozen trays of vegetables head towards the top of the tables.

'Now,' she said, and pulled Jack forward.

They stepped into the space between the two rows, just behind the Grenlick and keeping far enough back that she couldn't hear them or feel the air move around them. They moved halfway down the table before the Grenlick put the stack of trays on the left table, picked the stack up again minus the bottom tray and took two steps forward before repeating the process.

Claire suddenly felt uncomfortable, as though something was about to go wrong but she couldn't figure out what. Jack pulled on her arm. She ignored him at first, still trying to figure out what it was that felt so wrong, but when he tugged again – this time more urgently – she looked over her shoulder and choked back a gasp. A second Grenlick was entering the space behind them, servicing the other side of the tables. Claire had mistimed their entry.

The second Grenlick was moving more quickly. They were stuck in a sandwich. Claire moved them closer and closer to the girl in front; so close that Claire was sure she must be able to feel their body heat. Jack hugged closer and closer to Claire as the male worked his way down the table behind them. Trying to split her attention in both directions, Claire nearly stumbled into the Grenlick in front of her, and then she saw the male behind them was down to his last tray.

They were close to the end of the tables now. The girl still had two more trays to drop. Claire looked back. The male dropped his last tray, too early, but then gave it a push and slid it towards the chef waiting for it. Claire held her breath. Would he try to push past and bump into them? He looked, seemed to be judging the space and how easy it would be to get through, then he turned and walked back up the row. Claire struggled not to let out a huge sigh of relief, and she was sure she felt Jack's hand tremble in hers.

They repeated the process with the next table. Only one side was being used, and they could hurry along the gap when nobody was using it. The doors on this side were used more often too, and they didn't have to wait long before they could follow someone through. As soon as they were in past the doors, Claire slipped the goggles over her eyes, pinging the strap hard onto her ear with one-handed clumsiness. She didn't cry out - quite - but her eyes misted up, which was distinctly unhelpful.

Claire leaned against the wall for a moment. The absurdity of it all made it feel like she was playing a computer game. Some massive multi-user role playing extravaganza with stunning graphics. But there was no game, and that was what made her breath burn in her throat and her hands tingle. She closed her eyes for a moment to blink away the moisture then looked over her shoulder to see if Jack was ready. She realised that wasn't going to help as he couldn't see her eyes, so she gave his hand a squeeze, and got a jerky nod in reply. That made her feel guilty. He must have been scared, too, and he didn't have the comfort – if that was the right word – of being able to keep telling himself this was all for Evie. For a moment she wondered why he had come along, but pushed the thought away. They had a job to do.

The trail went along the corridor for a few yards, then turned off to the left. Claire set off, dragging Jack behind her. As soon as they turned away from the main corridor, everything got quieter. They turned another corner, then the trail took them up a narrow flight of stairs. The stairwell wasn't cramped, but it was more house-size than office-size. The stairs went farther up, but the trail came off at the first landing and doubled back more or less the way they had come.

The décor was a little better up here. The floor was still uncarpeted, but it looked as though it had been polished and there were fewer marks on the walls where trolleys had been crashed into them. The lighting, oddly, was worse. Downstairs, there had been long strip lights everywhere, like fluorescent tubes but still using magic. Here the lighting was from smaller fittings on the walls which left pools of shadow every few yards.

The trail took another turn and as Claire began to follow it around the corner she pulled up short and started pushing Jack back.

'What is it?'

'There are two mountainous Hrund up there, guarding a door.'

'How far?'

'Not sure. Ten yards?'

'And is that where Jones is?'

Claire felt her face go red. 'I don't know. I didn't check the trail. I just saw them and backed up.'

Jack looked thoughtful for a moment. 'Have another look, and see if there's space to get past them.'

Claire peered cautiously around the corner, afraid even though she knew they couldn't see her, then turned back to Jack. 'I might squeeze past, but I'm not sure you could. It's really narrow.'

'And the trail?'

Claire shook her head. 'I'm not sure.'

'Huh?'

'The trail goes along the corridor, but I can't see if it goes into the room. The guards are in the way.'

'So they might have brought her there, dropped her off, and carried on out the other way, or just gone through to somewhere else? Is that what you're saying?'

'Maybe.' Claire knew she sounded defensive, but what did he expect. She could only see what she could see. 'Should we use another distractor?'

'What are they?'

'One is screaming for help, and the other is a fake fire.'

Jack frowned. 'Either of them might bring people from all over the place. Opposite effect.'

'So what do we do?'

Jack rubbed his free hand over his mouth and jaw. To Claire, it looked like he had an idea but he didn't like it much. 'I have to draw them away,' he said at last, and Claire knew she didn't like the idea either. 'You can go on by yourself,' Jack explained. 'If she is in there, you can grab her and jump out. If she isn't – well, it's up to you if you follow the trail any further.'

Claire didn't look at him. Couldn't. This wasn't how it was supposed to happen. 'How will you get away from them?' If he couldn't, there was no way of knowing what they would do to him, officially or otherwise.

'I can mix in with a crowd, or jump out if it gets too tricky.'

'Jumping out takes time. Concentration.'

'I know. I'll make sure I stay well ahead of them. Just don't hang around when you find Jones. Shit, is she going to owe me some favours if we get her out of this.' His face lost some of its seriousness and a playful smile crept over his lips and up to his eyes as he looked at her. 'You, too.'

Claire felt her cheeks tingle and looked away. He didn't have to be doing this. Evie wasn't his friend, and she was pretty sure he still wasn't totally convinced Evie was in here. Was he doing this for her? Her head started to spin at the thought, and at how worried she was that something might happen to him. Without really thinking, she reached up with her free hand, put it behind his neck and pulled his face lower before she kissed him firmly on the lips. 'Be careful,' she said, letting go of his next before reaching into a pocket and pulling out a biro. Twisting their still clasped hands over, she started writing. 'For when you get out. Right out, to the Real. Text me, or something, so I know.'

Jack looked down at the digits written on the back of his hand. 'I may never wash this again, you know,' she said, and gave her an exaggerated wink. Claire resisted the temptation to use the pen to stab him in the arm, and settled for giving him a scowl. 'This is serious. Now, do you want one of the distractors?'

He seemed to think about it for a moment, then shook his head. 'You might need them. As soon as you see me run down the corridor, step over the other side. I don't want anyone crashing into you by accident. Ready?'

Claire wanted to say no. She wanted to find anything that would postpone the moment when she would be left on her own and Jack would run off with two angry Hrund snapping at his heels. She told herself off. She had already done things more dangerous, and more stupid. She looked up at Jack and nodded.

'Remember, move over there,' he pointed with his chin, then pulled his hand from hers and starting around the corner. She watched in horror as Jack ran directly towards the guards.

TWENTY EIGHT

Halfway down the corridor Jack seemed to notice the Hrund and slid to a stop. He hesitated, then made a terrible imitation of the 'black power' salute from the eighties. 'Capitalist thugs,' he shouted. 'Come on, come and get me, you gutless bastards. I'll never tell you where it is. Power to the revolution. You'll never find it before it goes off.'

The Hrund, who had been looking at Jack with idle curiosity, and no small amount of contempt, suddenly paid an awful lot more attention. One stepped towards Jack with hands peacefully raised. 'Hold on, sir. Are you telling me that—'

Jack was backing away. 'You'll never find all of them. Not in time. Even if you catch me, I won't tell you.'

He was nearly back to the junction now. One Hrund was only a half dozen steps from him, and the other was halfway between Jack and the door. Jack turned and ran. A split second later, so did the Hrund closest to him. The other walked up to the end of the narrow corridor and watched. He was so close Claire could have touched him, but he showed no sign of joining the chase. The plan was falling apart.

Claire put her hand into her pocket as she looked over her shoulder. The main passageway went on for a dozen yards then made a T-junction. She pulled both the remaining distractors out of her pocket, and played a gamble. Squeezing one to activate it, she touched it lightly to the back of the Hrund's tunic, where it stuck.

The countdown on this one was much shorter, only ten seconds. Tolks had told her that this device would make someone think they could hear a cry for help in the distance, and it would keep leading them away from wherever it was activated. She heard the faint cries start. The Hrund turned his head this way and that, as if trying to judge where the noise was coming from, his face taking on a concerned look. He fidgeted, looking nervously back towards the door, obviously worried about deserting his post. Claire heard the cries for help get more insistent, and at the last minute realised she was standing right in the path the guard was going to take. She stepped to the side as he started to move, and was on her way down to the door as soon as she was sure the Hrund wasn't going to turn back.

It was a very ordinary door; simple, cheap and with plain handles. There was no keyhole, but a bolt had been screwed untidily into placed about halfway up. Claire grabbed the bolt, pulled it back, and pushed the door open.

A wave of wrongness washed out just as she shifted her weight forward to step into the room. She stopped herself before she took a step, and peered inside. Evie was sitting on a chair in the middle of the room, looking at the door in confusion. Claire called out to her. Evie looked like she heard something but wasn't sure what and Claire remembered that the amulet dampened sound as well as sight. Her hands were already touching the cord to lift it off her neck when she hesitated. What if taking it off deactivated it? Would it switch back on? She let go of the thong and wracked her brains. She had to get Evie to come close enough to touch her, and that meant something Evie would trust. Claire pulled her goggles over her head and threw them.

Claire watched as Evie's eyes tracked them through the air. Her aim was better then she had expected and rather than landing on the floor at Evie's feet, the goggles landed in her lap. Evie picked them up, looked at them, then stared at the doorway, frowning. Her eyes and mouth slowly opened wide, and her hands came up, palms forward, as though pushing whomever was there away. 'Stop. Don't come in. The room is a magic trap.'

Claire was relieved she had felt the wrongness. Whatever it was might have broken something she was going to rely on. Instead, she willed Evie to get off her backside and hurry over. Evie did come to the door, but at a careful walk, and she seemed to be trying to peer around the edges of the door before she was even in the doorway. As soon as Evie's hand touched the doorframe, Claire placed her own hand over it. Evie squealed and snatched her hand away, then started laughing.

'I knew it would be you,' she said, holding her arms open. Claire rushed in and gave her a hug, and was surprised by how fiercely Evie held her in return. She was also surprised by how Evie looked. A little dishevelled, yes, but she looked clean and her clothes were exactly what Claire would have expected her to be wearing. Unless they were freshly laundered, there was something else going on.

'I knew none of those idle, brain-dead, useless... I just knew it would be you.' Evie said again as she relaxed the death-grip she had on Claire and held her out at arm's length. She noticed the amulet. 'Is that Grenlick?'

'Is now the time to worry?' Claire said. 'We have to get you out of here.' She changed things around until they were just holding hands and tugged.

'Wait,' said Evie. 'They may not even check.' She let go of Claire, pulled the door shut and pushed the bolt back, then groped around until Claire could catch her hand again. 'Right. That might buy us some time. Now we can go. Let's get away from here before we try to jump out. I don't like the way things feel.'

Claire led Evie back the way she had come, but when they got to the stairwell, Evie stopped, pulling Claire to a halt too.

Claire looked back and saw Evie was looking up the stairs, not down. 'What are you doing? We have to get out.'

'How long does this invisibility thing last?' Evie asked.

'No bloody idea and I would rather be outside before we find out.'

'I can't,' said Evie.

There was a silence that lasted a heartbeat. 'What?'

'I was investigating... something,' Evie explained. 'It's too complicated to go into now. They brought me here for a reason, but I think this is where they control whatever is going on. So where are we?'

'Stellar Cellar, and the place is crawling with people, so if we can just—'

'Natrak,' Evie clicked her fingers and looked very pleased with herself. 'I knew that scrawny vulture had something to do with all this. We have to find out more. Which floor are we on?'

'One up from the basement. Look, do we have time?' Claire was getting annoyed that Evie didn't seem that impressed with the rescue.

'Let's make it. I'll never get this chance again. I've been sat in that room for hours and I want some payback. We have to find his office, or close enough to it so I can jump back in here later.'

'How can we find that? We have no idea of the layout of the place.'

'We can make a good guess,' said Evie, pulling Claire to go up the stairs. 'Underland is a parasite. It steals from the Real, copies it, and hates change. Think of every nightclub you've seen in an old movie. What's the layout?'

Claire thought for a moment. 'The boss' office looks out over the club from above.'

Evie grinned and they carried on up the stairs.

The stairway ended at a plain door. There was no window, and Evie opened it very slowly. Claire flinched when she pulled the door wide open. 'It's OK. Nobody there,' she said over her shoulder as she dragged Claire through.

206

The corridor was positively plush, if tacky. Thick red carpet muffled their footsteps. The walls were covered with heavy fabric wallpaper in an even darker red, with a pattern embossed in black. Light came from ornate fittings on the walls, all dripping fake crystals like mini-chandeliers, or from equally dangly ceiling fittings surrounded by fancy plaster medallions.

Claire was starting to feel like unappreciated baggage, or a convenient rack to hang the invisibility amulet on as Evie pulled her along the short corridor to the next junction. 'Evie. This is crazy. Let's get out of here.'

'Soon.' Evie stopped and turned to face Claire. 'Look, I know this seems nuts, but I'm onto something. Something really important. If I just leave all I'll have is suspicions and questions. If I can get into his office I can maybe get answers.'

'Is that why you didn't jump out?'

'What? No. Don't be stupid. There's something weird about that room. You can't jump. I tried for hours.'

She started to turn away, but Claire pulled her back. She had realised that Evie thought she had only been locked in the room for a few hours, full stop. Something had been playing with her sense of time. 'And you want me to risk getting caught and stuck in here too? They have the police looking for you in the Real, Evie. You've been gone for nearly *two weeks*.'

Evie looked shaken, but then her face went back to her 'resolved' look. 'We can sort all that out later. Look, if you want to bail, give me whatever kit you have and jump.'

Claire nearly slapped her, and considered the suggestion for several seconds before rejecting it. 'Not yet.' She gave Evie's hand a harsh shake. 'But don't think I won't, and don't think I'll bother waiting around to swap amulets with you or give you your Kevlar back if I decide to go. This is really stupid.' Evie nodded, then turned and led the way to the junction. Claire followed, still not quite sure why, still trembling angry.

The next corridor was as tastefully decorated as the first. To the left, both sides of the corridor had doors every few feet. To the right, only one side was so heavily populated. The other had only two doors. 'That way,' said Evie. 'The rest are private rooms.'

Claire wondered why a nightclub would need private rooms, and so many of them. And why Evie had put such a funny verbal twist on the word 'private'. Then her face burned like a bonfire and she tried not to think about it anymore.

Evie walked to the closer of the two doors and put her ear to it. She flinched away, turning back to Claire and putting a finger to her lips before moving on to the next door. Claire assumed she had heard voices from within and said nothing, even though she wanted to scream at Evie it was time to go. At the next door Evie listened, then listened some more before she gently tried the handle. The door clicked softly as it opened, and there was a soft hiss as it rubbed across the carpet. Once they were inside Evie closed the door and twisted the lock before she let go of Claire's hand.

The office was as tasteful as the corridor outside. The desk was oversized and richly inlaid with complicated veneers, and behind it was a huge, overstuffed leather chair on rollers. Two lesser chairs were in front of the desk, obviously designed to show who the boss was, and there was a small table with four more chairs set off to one side. It was a room for doing business in, not entertaining. Two of the walls were little more than long windows. The ones that looked out over the club had vertical blinds, pulled closed. The wall between this room and the room with voices had a door, and all the windows had slat blinds. The wood had a reddish texture to it, like pale mahogany. All the blinds were closed.

Evie picked up one of the guest chairs and propped it under the handle of the connecting door before turning to the desk and starting to rummage through the papers. Claire hadn't a clue what she should look for, so she stayed out of the way. Still invisible, it would be just their luck that Evie would bump into her and knock something over.

Instead, Claire walked to the window looking over the club and gently spread two of the leaves. It was an impressive view.

The décor was still cheesy red and black, and from here she could see the long bar and most of the floor. It was still early, and very quiet. Where there was obviously supposed to be a band, a pianist and a double-bass filled in for mood music. A few of the booths were occupied; some with self-contained groups, others with one or two men being kept company by 'hostesses'.

Two of the hostesses were Hrund, and there were no Grenlix. The rest were tall and willowy and buxom and looked like femmes fatale in skin tight sheath dresses and towering heels. Again, the dominant colour scheme was fire-engine red, with a preponderance of dark hair. They didn't look human, but Claire wasn't sure what race they did come from. She did notice they all sat about as far away from each other as they could, and that there was a lot of mutual glowering going on.

She turned back to see what Evie was doing. She was still looking through the papers on the desk, though her expression suggested she hadn't found anything of use to her yet. She let the last bundle of papers fall back more or less where she taken them from, and she turned to look at the larger table. Claire's shoulders slumped. How much longer? She turned away to look out the window again, but Evie chose that moment to let out a gasp. At the same time, the noise level from the room next door increased. It might have been laughter, and it didn't sound alarmed, but Claire looked back to the table and saw Evie was alert too. She was halfway through folding up a large sheet of paper. After a moment, she carried on, stuffing the sheet into a pocket and reaching for another. With her other hand, she touched a finger to her eye and pointed to the window between the two rooms. Claire figured Evie wanted her to see what was going on next door.

She walked over to the wooden blind, the soft sound of folding paper behind her, and studied the problem. How could she move the blind? Nobody within would see her, but if anyone looked up, they would see the blinds twisted out of line. She edged back and forth, looking for a gap that would let her see

209

what was going on. The gap was there but it was small and didn't let her see much; the back of one person, who could have been an Angel, and the face of another. Claire frowned. Not Grenlick, Angel, Hrund or Sathaari, and as soon as she saw him she felt a wrongness, like a soft echo of whatever had been done to Evie's prison.

Not quite sure why, Claire held her goggles up to her eyes, but almost dropped them when she looked through. The mysterious man glowed like fresh Morph-trail. Claire knew she hadn't made any noise, and she knew she hadn't touched the blind, but at the instant she looked through the goggles, the strange being looked directly at her. Directly. Eye to eye contact. An instant later she felt a curious sensation, like a bubble around her popping, and knew she had just become visible.

TWENTY NINE

'Evie,' she called, trying to keep her voice low. As she spoke the creature in the other room spoke to the Angel. 'They know we're here.' As the Angel rose from his seat, turning, the creature again made eye contact with Claire again and she felt the same terrible wrongness that had saturated the room Evie had been in. 'Get out,' Claire yelled. 'We can't jump.'

The Angel was already at the connecting door, rattling the handle and pushing the door against the chair Evie had propped in front of it. Claire turned, heading for the other door, and saw Evie was frozen in the act of stuffing yet another oversize sheet of paper into a pocket. 'Out. Now.'

Claire made one of the hardest decisions of her life and set off without Evie. If they were both caught, then there was only Jack. If he was caught too, nobody would ever come looking for any of them. She threw the office door open and went out into the corridor. Looking out from a different angle, Claire saw that the last door had a sign above it saying 'To the Club'. It wasn't a room. It was a stairwell. Her hand was already in her pocket, fingers activating the last distractor as she pulled it out and tossed it right in front of the door to the other office. Dense smoke billowed out, looking thick enough to walk on, and filled the width of the corridor in seconds. Claire took a last look over her shoulder. The smoke was almost to the office door, and Evie was just coming out. She gave her one more chance. 'This way. Come on.'

She didn't wait, but pushed through the door. The stairwell was better decorated, obviously for customers and not staff, with carpeted stairs and moody lighting. Claire ran at the stairs and heard the door crash open again before she was halfway down the first flight. Alarm bells started to ring all over the club. As she reached the doors at the bottom, she heard Evie yell to her from above. 'Make for the front doors. Go with the punters.' Without answering, Claire pulled a door open and ran out onto the floor of the club.

For the first four or five steps, time seemed to slip into slow motion and detail flooded into her from all around. The pianist and the bass player were still performing, but looking worried. The hostesses were ushering what customers there were towards a double door at the other end of the room and the barman was taking the cash tray out of his till. Hrund bouncers near the exit saw her, but made no move to intercept her. The doors behind her crashed open again, presumably as Evie came through. Claire looked up to the gallery. The enraged face of an Angel looked down on her next to the calm and slightly amused expression of the unknown monster. She stumbled to a stop, time returning to normal, and pulled her eyes away from the gallery just in time to see a Morph's tongue shooting towards her head.

Claire tried to duck and turn. Not her whole body, only her head. The Kevlar took the blow, spreading it out across the top half of her body but she was still knocked from her feet and thrown backwards towards the bar. Her head rang. Everything looked like it was in 3-D and she had forgotten her glasses. To her right came a dimly heard 'No' and the noise of furniture breaking. Claire sat up, shook her head gently and looked around. A pair of hidden doors had opened in the wall below the gallery. Two Morphs were sliming across the club, one towards her, the other towards Evie. Evie was throwing chairs at both of them, trying to distract them while Claire was on the ground. The bouncers were still out of the way at the main door and showed no interest in getting involved.

She fumbled at her leg for her PPG, but the holster clip was still in place. As she tugged at it to release it, a Morph got close enough to attack. Its mouth opened as the clip came off, but Claire knew she would never get the gun out or the safety off in time. She froze; waiting, watching, lifting her centre of balance forward onto the balls of her feet, tensing her muscles. Russian roulette. Penalty kick. At the slightest twitch of movement in the Morph's mouth she threw herself to the left.

The tongue, fist, nasty hard thing went by so close she was sure she felt a draft, but she didn't stop moving. She knew it took them several seconds to 'reload' and she wanted to be out of range by then, or behind cover. She rolled to her feet and ran alongside the bar for a half dozen paces, then jumped onto it and rolled to the other side. As soon as she landed she crouched and pulled the PPG out of its holster. Her thumb flipped the safety off and she glanced down to check the charge. Full. Her head popped up over the bar as she took a quick sight on the Morph closest to her and fired. She didn't wait to see if she hit anything. She dropped behind the bar again and started to crawl.

There was a crash from somewhere in front of her, and Claire's first thought was that Evie had been hit. When she got to the other end of the bar, she poked her head out until she could see what was going on. Both Morphs were now attacking Evie, and she was being herded into a corner. Perfect. Claire moved herself a little farther out so that she could get a clear shot, and concentrated took her time to aim.

She fired twice at the Morph closest to Evie then, while the shots were still in the air, she adjusted her aim and fired two more shots into the second. On the fourth shot the gun made a strange cough, and the last cloud didn't look right, but it didn't matter. Both Morphs exploded into puddles of slippery goo. Evie picked her way through the mess and ran to take cover with

213

Claire. 'Let's get out of here.'

Claire nodded and started to wrap herself in the intention of leaving, but something still interfered. She couldn't jump. She opened her mouth to tell Evie, but saw from the anger and confusion on her friends face that she, too, was having a problem. Evie held out her hand. 'Let me see that damned gun.'

Claire handed it over. Evie turned it on its side. Claire gasped and Evie looked somehow defeated. The charge crystal showed the gun was empty, which was impossible. The gun was supposed to hold charge for six shots and, even for this earlier, less efficient model, it should have been able to recharge enough for two more shots by now.

'What do we do?' Claire asked.

Evie looked thoughtful for a moment. 'If I only we knew what was stopping us jumping.'

Claire pointed to the observation window. 'Up there. With the Angel. I don't know what he, it, is, but I think he's causing it.'

'Then let's get as far away from him as we can. Crawl down to the other end of the bar. We can rush the bouncers and get out with the crowd.'

Claire did as Evie suggested. She didn't think the crowd was big enough to hide in but it was the best idea they had. When she got to the other end she could see people, hostesses, and no bouncers. She stood up, ready to hurry over to the small crowd still pushing to get through the doors and away from the violence.

She had only taken two steps when a Hrund bouncer stepped out from behind one of the main doors, twenty feet in front of her. He had a hand-bow in his right hand and was holding his left hand out, palm forward. 'Stop right there. Put your weapon on the ground, and kick it away.'

Claire looked down and realised that she had, quite automatically, lined the PPG up with the bouncer's chest. Even if there had been enough charge in it to actually fire, she doubted it could hurt him. She wondered if he knew that. Hand-bows, which were basically miniature crossbows, were single

214

shot. The string had to be pulled back and a new quarrel fitted each time they were fired. Admittedly, his looked odd, but maybe that was because it was unlicensed and illegal. Her weapons training told her a hand-bow couldn't penetrate a Kevlar.

'No, drop yours, or I'll fire,' she said, trying to sound like she meant it. The Hrund's eyes narrowed and Claire tried to make out if he was doubting her or the weapon. Or both. If she could get him to shoot at her, then his weapon would be useless and they could get past him and get out. She twitched her PPG up, as if firing it. The Hrund fired too.

The little quarrel slammed into her right shoulder, knocking her backward a half-step. Her arm swung outwards, throwing the useless PPG across the club, and she twisted her balance back again, ready to run forward.

The second quarrel hit her other shoulder, and she staggered back another step, pushing Evie back and sideways. What other quarrel? There shouldn't have been another. As she looked back at the bouncer, she saw another round already loaded in the hand-bow. That was impossible. Did he have more than one? There was another dull twang and the bolt took Claire in the centre of her chest.

She fell backward, Evie's Kevlar burning her skin, dragging glasses and bottles from the back of the bar. She looked up at the Hrund. He had stepped closer, was looming over her. He had a savage grin, and a wide, wild look in his eyes and Claire knew he was going to fire again. How was he reloading so fast? The hand-bow played another deep note and Claire cried out. The amulet stung her skin and the bolt thumped into her shoulder; not hard enough to cut through her heavy coat, but enough so she knew she would bruise.

'Stop,' Evie screamed, close to her. 'Can't you see her Kevlar is down? We surrender.'

But the bouncer had taken another step closer, and his eyes still shone with some ugly delight in what he was doing and his hand came up to point the weapon at Claire's head and his finger

215

started to tighten on the trigger and with a last shriek of 'No!' Evie was in the air and between the bouncer and Claire.

The thrum of the hand-bow was followed by a sickening, meaty, *thwock*, Evie seemed to fall faster towards Claire, a look of agonised surprise on her face. She landed hard and Claire's arms instinctively folded around her friend. As the bouncer raised his weapon again, Claire demanded to be somewhere else. She didn't care where, and she didn't care when, but she reached into that place she used when she needed to jump, fighting past whatever it was that was trying to stand in her way, grabbed hold of the Real and pulled.

THIRTY

As soon as they arrived wherever it was she had taken them, Claire's mobile started howling for attention. Evie tried to lift herself off Claire, but screamed and fell back.

'Can you hold yourself up on your other arm,' Claire gasped, Evie's weight robbing her of breath. 'Maybe I can slide out and help you up.'

Evie didn't say anything, but Claire saw muscles ripple along the line of her jaw. A moment later and the weight lifted off her chest. She slid sideways and rolled to her knees, turning to help take Evie's weight. As they struggled to their feet, Evie started to laugh, weakly, balancing uncontrollable humour against the pain of the quarrel sticking out of her right shoulder.

'Can't jump, eh?' Evie said, her voice thin.

Claire looked up, frowned, and shook her head in disbelief. Across the road was the entrance to Chaine Farm Hospital A&E department. The last time she had been here was five years ago when she had cracked a bone in her wrist. She had jumped them to within thirty feet of the doors.

As they waited to cross the road to the door of the A&E, Claire realised they had a problem. 'Why are we here?' Evie picked up on the problem straight away. 'Oh crap. We don't

217

have any time and I can't think straight. You'll have to come up with something.'

'Me? Again? That's not fair.'

Evie mixed laughing and groaning in roughly equal measure as they crossed the road and Claire was forced to join in. There was a perverse irony to it. 'You can't remember a thing,' she said after a moment's thought. 'Me and my boyfriend found you wandering at the side of the road. He couldn't wait.'

'You don't have a boyfriend,' Evie argued. They had reached the other side of the road and she was working her good hand around her coat, picking out folded sheets of paper and Underland contraband. Claire tried to hide them as fast as they were handed to her.

'I can get one.'

'In five minutes?'

'Hope so.'

Evie chuckled again, but this time her knees seemed to lose interest in keeping her upright and Claire had to grab her arm and help steady her. A passing nurse noticed them, saw the blood running from Evie's back and rushed over. Then the NHS took over and Evie was whisked away on a wheelchair.

Claire was shown to a waiting room and an eagle-eyed nurse outside watched to make sure she didn't break out and try to make a run for it. She caught a frown as she fiddled with her mobile, but she was too tired to care. There were ten missed calls and twelve texts, and it was only then that she realised she hadn't snapped back. The same time she had spent in Underland had passed in the Real; it was now very late in the evening and she had mysteriously disappeared from home before dinner. That was the first thing to sort out. She dialled home, and after 'Hello, mum,' spent the better part of five minutes listening to her mother having minor hysterics before she could get a word though in any direction let alone sideways.

'Mum, listen. I need you to come and pick me up.'

'Where are you? What's happened? I'm calling the polic–'

'Mum, I don't have much battery left. Can you come and get

218

me? I'm at the Chaine Farm A and E–'

'Ohmygod, ohmygod, ohmygod, whatever has happened are you hurt ohmyg-'

'I'm fine. Totally. Look, can you just come get me and I'll explain everything when you get here.'

She pushed the button to disconnect the call, prayed that her father would be driving, and started looking through the texts. The first six were from her mother or father, as were the last five. The seventh made her break out in a huge smile of relief.

Claire opened the message from the unknown number.

The entry simply said 'Safe', but she knew who it was from. She saved the number against the name 'Jack' and sent a text back.

'You are now officially my boyfriend. Explain later.'

She deleted both the inbound and outbound texts.

Her parents turned up moments before the police, who had been called by the hospital as soon as they had realised that Evie was the girl who had been reported missing. Questions were asked, but Claire stuck to the simplest lie. She and a boyfriend her parents didn't know about – because she didn't think they would approve of him – had been driving around and had seen a girl stumbling down the street. They had slowed, seen she was injured, stopped and offered to take her to the hospital, which was nearby. The girl had seemed confused, and didn't know her name or where she was. Her boyfriend couldn't spend hours hanging around the hospital, so he had dropped them at the A&E and gone home, while Claire had helped the girl inside.

Nobody was entirely happy with the story, but there was nothing to disprove it, and eventually Claire was allowed to go home. She sat on the back seat. Her mother was babbling, her father concentrating on the road, and the slightly too warm air seduced her already exhausted body. She twisted around until she was lying on her side, knees bent, arms folded in front of her. She ached, she was going to have a monster bruise on her shoulder, and she was deeply weary. As she watched the streetlights flash by overhead, she pushed aside all the thoughts and questions that still rattled around her head. She could deal with them another day. For now, she had been right. She had told them Evie had been captured, and had even rescued her. They would have to reinstate her. As her eyelids became too heavy to hold up, she started to smile.

She was still Warrior Stone.

WHITE MAGIC

WARRIOR STONE: BOOK 2

All is not well in Underland

Human Observers are being replaced by Grenlix, and humans are losing their memories.

Claire is being taught magic, which no human should be able to do. Somebody is not happy about this, and about Claire poking her nose into what's behind the missing memories

Things, nasty things, start to happen to Claire and to those around her.

Visit www.metaphoric-media.co.uk for ordering information

Aphrodite's Dawn

Garret's world is six floors tall by five hundred people wide, and when a voice in his head offers him and escape from his boring life, he has no idea how much being offered everything he could want is going to change him.

His universe is thrown into chaos when he discover he lives on an asteroid-sized sleeper-ship. The crew is missing, the computer has been damaged, and the only way they can reach their new home is if Garret takes a message to the other end of the world.

Visit www.metaphoric-media.co.uk for ordering information

MAVERICK

(AS ROBERT HARKESS)

They settled their world hundreds of years ago, turning their backs on technology, closing the Gate behind them. When their children began to develop impossible powers they rejoiced and called them Golden – until they took over. Now the Golden are feared.

Elanor comes to her powers not as a child, but as a young woman – a Maverick. The Golden are rumoured to do terrible things to Mavericks, so Elanor runs.

Anatol has travelled from the home world, decades of suspended animation, to stop the Gate malfunctioning and destroying both worlds.

He and Elanor collide, and form an uneasy truce of science and magic.

Visit www.metaphoric-media.co.uk for ordering information

Made in the USA
Charleston, SC
01 February 2016